OUR RIVER JORDAN

JACKSON OWEN

JACKSON OWEN

Printed Worldwide
First Printing 2025
First Edition 2025

ISBN: 979-8-9931768-0-2 (Paperback)
ISBN: 979-8-9931768-1-9 (Hardcover)

10 9 8 7 6 5 4 3 2 1

Interior Book Design by Walt's Book Design
www.waltsbookdesign.com

OUR RIVER
JORDAN

DEDICATION

Our River Jordan, my first novel, is dedicated to my beautiful children, Catherine Grace and John Henry. My greatest wish is that you willfully stand in the gap for those who can't stand. I will have fallen short as a Father if you do not feel called to bend a knee and show the love of Christ to someone who needs it. I pray that you become warriors for Christ and never forget where it all started: behind our house, with our feet in the cool water of the Pintlala Creek.

TABLE OF CONTENTS

PREFACE

Years ago, my father's old friend, Sam Henry, passed away. I tagged along to the funeral to pay my respects to a special man whom I had grown to love. Each deer season, when our freezers were full of venison, I would donate each deer to Sam and his family. We grew close, and the stories that he shared with me about my grandfather, a man I never met, gave me closure. When my father, uncle, and I arrived at the funeral, I quickly realized we were the only white people in attendance. I wondered how they would treat us. Immediately, Sam Henry's brother, Tom, walked us to the front of the church, and everyone there treated us like we were family. After the funeral, the kindness and generosity that were extended to my family made me realize how much better this world would be if we loved one another, despite our differences. I learned that Sam's father, Joe Jones, lived on our property at one time. I began to dig and research the history of my family and the immediate area I grew up in. Using real names from an ancestor's family Bible, this fictional story was born. While it is a fiction novel, Our River Jordan is inspired by real people, places, and events. Some names have been changed or altered.

Acknowledgement

I would like to thank God for hearing my prayers and planting this seed. To my family and friends, thank you for allowing me to dream. Also, I would like to thank Karen Dieckmann for believing in me and coming alongside me during this process.

EPIGRAPH

For we were all baptized by one Spirit so as to form one body—whether Jews or Gentiles, slave or free—and we were all given the one Spirit to drink.

1 Corinthians 12:13 NIV

1

John Harrison-1959

William McCrae had been a bully for as long as I had known him. Every day after school, he tormented his victims on the bus. I guess, even at an early age, some kids can feel entitled because of what their last name is. William's family was extremely wealthy, and he never wanted for anything. His father gave him what he wanted when he wanted it, and he didn't take no for an answer. I was convinced that he was never held accountable because of the family that he belonged to.

I knew in my heart that William pushed people around because no other young man had called his bluff, but my father taught me from an early age to never fight unless it was to protect myself or my family. My younger sister Anna and I had very few friends because of my family's reputation. We were not popular like William by any means, but our family was feared and respected for reasons that I did not yet know. Anna sat beside me on the bus, and for the most part, the kids who stayed in trouble left us alone.

I looked forward to the bus ride home from school because it meant that I could spend the remainder of the evening exploring our property and escaping reality. I tried to keep my mind fixed on the freedom that I felt in the woods to block out the negativity around me. For some reason, the slow rides down the winding country roads were peaceful. Normally, I was able to block out the noise around me and mind my own business like my father had taught me to do. Despite trying my best, one day, both my patience and my discipline were tested on that bus.

William was feeling brave that Friday on the way home from school, and that would put him and me both in a pickle. He confidently came and sat down behind us and began to bully my sister. I knew that it was his way of indirectly pushing my buttons. We were not friends, and I usually steered clear of him in fear of what I might do if he treated me the way that he treated everyone else. Unlike William, I knew that after a bad day, I would have to answer to my father when I got home. It seemed that we were about to get to know each other very well as he kept pestering Anna from the seat behind us.

"Hey, Anna, I heard your folks were nigger lovers. My old man has told me all about it," William said. His friends joined in by laughing and making the situation worse. I placed my hand on Anna's shoulder to remind her that she wasn't alone. I was doing my best to detach from the problem, but when I saw a tear roll down my sister's cheek, a familiar feeling came over me.

I could feel my body tensing up and my chest getting tight. My blood started rushing to my head, and I could not contain myself any longer. I spun around in my seat and said, "William, leave her alone or you are about to have a bad day!"

William then laughed and said, "What are you going to do about it? Your little nigger friend isn't here to protect you." The bus got quiet, and all eyes were locked on me. All I could think about was my father grounding me and not being able to deer hunt after school.

I wasn't willing to sacrifice my time in the woods, so I turned back around and settled in my seat. William then leaned up and whispered in my ear, "That's what I thought, coward." Before the word coward had finished rolling from his lips, I snapped. I threw my right elbow back and caught him square in the nose. Before he could react, I quickly jumped up and closed the distance between us. I could see the blood pouring from his nose as he tried to catch it in his hands.

I dragged him to the floor between the seats and got on top of him. The first couple of blows were all emotional and misguided as I connected with the floor of the bus. After I got him pinned down with my knees, I landed a few good shots to his face. When I felt him give up, reality set in, and something told me to ease up. I got up and looked at my sister, and she had a look on her face that I had never seen. It was a look of fear and amazement. She jumped up, hugged me, and clung to my side.

The bus driver, Miss Rhonda Bibb, called me to the front of the bus, and Anna followed. Miss Rhonda was a rather large, colored lady who lived on Cruise Road, not a stone's throw from our place. She knew my family, and she knew William's family. Her father and grandfather worked alongside mine in the cornfield and pea patch every summer. She called me up to where she was driving and said, "I've been waiting for somebody to handle that boy. I'm just glad you got to him before I did. Lord knows I can't lose my job because of who his daddy is." I had feared that she was going to have me kicked out of school, but I was relieved to know that she was on my side.

When the bus turned onto Mason Road, my sister and I prepared to get off the bus. My adrenaline had worn off, and I was thinking clearly again. In a way, I felt bad for William because he hadn't said a word since the fight. Something told me to go make things right with him before the weekend.

I walked back in his direction, holding eye contact with him the entire time. His freckled face and his name-brand clothes were covered in dry blood. I knew that William's father, Billy, would be having a word with my dad soon. As I approached him, I started to apologize, and he said, "This isn't over. Wait until I tell my dad."

I replied, "Yeah, I couldn't imagine that you would let your daddy fight all of your battles." Afterwards, I walked back to the front of the bus and accepted the fact that I was in for a long weekend.

As Anna and I got off the bus, I spat on my knuckles and tried to rub the blood on my denim jeans. The deep throbbing pain in my right hand was a reminder of what I was about to face. I knew there was going to be hell to pay when Dad found out. I cautiously approached the house, hoping that he was not home yet. When I saw his old blue Chevrolet parked around the right side of the house, my heart dropped, and I started to think about what I would tell him.

I was born and raised just south of Montgomery, Alabama, in the Hope Hull community. Our house was down a short dirt road that turned left off Mason Road. The home that we lived in had been in our family for quite some time. It was passed down to my dad when my grandfather died just before I was born. Mama was usually on the front porch in her swing waiting for us to get home, and Dad was usually working on something around back if he was home. It wasn't a very spectacular home, but it was built by my grandfather and a couple of his friends. It was all I knew, and I was proud to live on our family land.

We had family members spread out within a quarter of a mile from our house. You could see two other houses from our old wooden wrap-around porch. My uncle, my father's identical twin, lived across the hayfield from us. The twins were always there for one another. It seemed like they could read each other's minds, and they had a very rare, close relationship.

As Anna and I came up on the front porch, I saw my mother, Sarah, on the swing. In an attempt to hide my clothes from her, I tried to go inside without speaking. Just as I opened the old screen door, I heard, "John Harrison, where do you think you are going?" I turned around slowly, knowing what was about to happen. Mama's eyes got as big as I had ever seen them when she saw that my shirt and jeans were covered in blood.

She asked what happened, and before I could tell her, Anna said, "Mama, he was just protecting me. It was my fault."

I couldn't let her take the blame for what I had done, so I cautiously went and sat down beside Mama on the swing. Mama was a very pretty lady with tan skin, long blonde hair, and blue eyes. She was full of love, but she could also be as mean as a hornet if she needed to be.

"I don't see any cuts or bruises on you, so please tell me that is not someone else's blood," she said. She saw my knuckles and knew that I had been in a fight. She asked me what happened so she would know what to tell Dad if he asked. I told her exactly what happened and did not leave anything out because I knew they would get a different story from Mr. McCrae when he told them.

She asked me if I had gotten in trouble, and I told her Miss Bibb had taken my side in the altercation. Mama also knew William and the McCrae family, and she knew William wasn't a saint by any means. I think she understood why I got into a fight, but she still made it a point to tell me how disappointed she was. I think her way of punishing me was to tell me that I had to go find Dad and tell him before dinner.

Dinner was a peaceful time for our family, and the table was a place to be thankful and talk about positive things. Before I could argue, she said, "You'd better go ahead and tell him now and get it over with. It's just going to be worse if he thinks you're trying to hide it from him. "

Anna tried to follow me as I walked down the wooden steps of our front porch. I told her to stay with Mama and that I could handle it. As I came around the corner, I could hear Dad cutting something with a handsaw. I could see a gambrel moving back and forth by the skinning shed, so I knew that he had killed a deer.

I kicked the gravel rocks approaching the skinning shed, and I heard the saw stop cutting. "What are you doing, boy? Did you have a good day at school?"

I knew he was in a good mood, so that made it a little easier to break the news to him. "Well, yes, sir. I had a good day at school, but I got in a fight with William on the bus ride home." He stood up off of one knee, wiped the sweat from his face with his bloody hand, and said, " You did what, son? Come here and sit down." My heart was beating hard in my chest, but I mustered the courage to go sit down by him on his tailgate.

My dad, Henry, wasn't a big man, but there was something about him that was quite intimidating. His body was built by hard manual labor. His grip strength was out of this world from twisting wrenches and working with his hands his entire life. Often we joked with him, telling him that he was "like a bull in a China shop." He never slowed down long enough to pay us any attention. He always had a goal and a vision to attain it. The only time he ever slowed down was when he slept. To me, as a young boy, it seemed that he was more of a machine than a man. He was tough as nails and had been through things that I was confident would have killed a lesser man.

I tried to lighten him up by asking him about the nice eight-point buck that was swinging in front of me. He said, "You don't worry about that deer until after you tell me why your clothes are covered in blood." I told him that I was just protecting Anna and that William was picking on her. "That McCrae boy?" he asked.

I replied, "Yes, sir."

Then he asked me why I thought fighting was the answer, and I reminded him that he told me it was okay to fight for our family. "Well, I guess I did tell you that, son, and your Grandaddy told me and your uncle the same thing," he said.

I felt convicted to tell him that protecting Anna was not the only reason that I had lost my temper. "Dad, William called me a coward right before the fight, and that is what set me off. His arrogance was too much for me to handle. I'm not sure what happened. I just blacked out."

"I would have done the same thing if someone was picking on your aunt Catherine and calling me a coward," he replied. I felt great relief when I didn't sense Dad getting angry with me.

He then made his way back over to the deer and began cutting through the thick bone of the deer's chest. The saw quickly removed more bone with each violent stroke. After that, he began to meticulously skin the deer out, and I could tell he wanted to say something that he wasn't saying. After a long moment of awkward silence, he said, "You know, fighting isn't always the answer, son, but you get it honestly. Your granddaddy was that way when it came to his family, and he passed that down to us. You know, you remind me so much of him, and I hate that you never got to meet him. Now go inside and wash up for dinner. Help your mother set the table, and we will talk about what your punishment will be later." I thought that I was off the hook, but I knew deep down that he couldn't just let it slide.

After Dad told me about his successful hunt, I made my way back to the house, went inside, and got ready to wash up. I could smell the food cooking in the kitchen, and I knew that Mama had made her famous fried okra. That was a smell I would never forget. After I came out, I threw my bloody clothes in the basket by the back door and made my way into the kitchen.

Mama did her best to take care of us when it came to cooking, and she never cooked anything that I wasn't crazy about. It was usually fresh vegetables from the garden and venison or fish from the Pintlala Creek, depending on what time of year it was. Mama didn't like to go to town much because she liked to keep to herself around the house most of the time. She loved people, but I don't guess she ever had much of a reason to leave our place. I think what mattered the most to her could be found right there on that piece of property.

She was born and raised in a prominent family just north of us in Montgomery, but unfortunately, her parents died before I could meet them. Dad said her siblings fought over the inheritance until there was nothing left. He had financially supported her since before I was born. She was always somewhat of a hermit, but Dad said it was just because she was so content with what God had given her. She loved the Lord more than anyone that I knew.

I was sitting by the fireplace reading one of Dad's trapping magazines when I heard him come up the back steps and knock the mud off his boots. I knew it was time to eat and talk about what my punishment would be. Dad came in and washed his hands, and splashed some water on his face. "Sarah, is that fried okra that I smell?" Mama smiled from ear to ear and confirmed that we would be having fried venison cubed steak with mashed potatoes and fried okra. I think that was my father's favorite time of day when he could come in and sit down with his family to eat.

Anna and I helped Mama with the food and got the table set for dinner. When we all sat down, Dad said a prayer and thanked the Lord for providing us with a freezer full of venison and for our family. Dad was a hardworking man, but he kept the Lord first in his life, and he wanted all of us to do the same. I think he had learned from his father and grandfather that he needed to set the right example for us.

The fried okra was fresh out of the grease and too hot to eat. As I stared at my plate, I thought about all of the work that went into this meal. Mama had battered the okra in cornmeal and fried it until it was crispy. Dad had taken a big, mature doe a couple of weeks before, and Mama had pulled the okra and potatoes from our garden the previous planting season. Anna and I didn't like to help Mama can all of our vegetables to preserve them, but we sure didn't mind eating them.

As the food cooled off, we all enjoyed the fruits of our labor in silence. Then Dad spoke up, "So what are we going to do about this deal with William McCrae?"

Mama replied, "Henry, we can talk about that later. "Dad said, "No, I think it is important for John to know that I think he did the right thing. He stood up for someone that he loved, and there is nothing wrong with that".

I was once again relieved, but that relief was short-lived when he said, "But he is still going to wake up at daylight and help me cut those trees on the North end for firewood." My heart sank when I realized that I wouldn't be able to deer hunt the next morning, but if helping Dad would bring an end to all of this trouble, then I was okay with that. He was a disciplinarian, and he believed that there was always a lesson to be learned in any situation.

The next morning, I felt a strong tug on my foot at the end of the bed. I ignored it and dozed back off, but I awoke suddenly when I felt my body being drug towards the end of the bed. My behind hit the wooden footboard at the end of the bed, and I sat up quickly. After I gathered myself, I could see Dad walking out of my room. It was time to eat breakfast and go to work.

My father had taught me how to work hard from a young age. That is the way he was raised, and I think he took pride in being a hard worker. Dad agreed with how I stood up for my sister, but I understood why he was doing what he was doing. I believe he was teaching me about making sacrifices and being a servant like Jesus Christ. Also, I don't imagine he wanted to handle working on those trees by himself.

After I got dressed and made my way into the living room, I saw Dad reading his Bible and drinking a cup of coffee by the fire. When I saw his thick flannel shirt, I knew that it had to be cold outside. He told me to go back into my room and put on some warmer clothes. Afterwards, I asked him what was for breakfast, and he said that we would be skipping breakfast because he wanted Mama to be able to sleep late. He assured me that by the time we took a break from working, she would be awake and have breakfast ready for us.

We eased out of the front door without being too loud, and I realized that the sun was not even up yet. It was just light enough to see where I was walking, and there was a layer of frost on the wooden porch steps. I followed Dad out to the barn, where he started the truck to let it warm up. We went to the old horse stall in the barn and got two chainsaws and multiple chains. By this time, I could already feel the cold nipping at my face and the wind cutting through my thin gloves.

We loaded the equipment in the bed of Dad's truck and made the loop around the house to the driveway. None of my cousins was awake yet. I knew that because there were no lights on in any of the three houses on our place. I thought about how nice it would be to be in my warm bed under the blankets, but my thoughts were interrupted when Dad spoke up. "I taught you how to run that chainsaw last summer. Do you think you can still handle it?"

"Yes, sir, I can still run it. You'll see."

Truthfully, I was always trying to impress my dad. I looked up to him and respected him so much that I wanted to be just like him. There were so many things that he could do that seemed far out of reach for me. I was always in awe and always eager to learn. He had a way of making me feel like there was always room for improvement in any task that I performed. I'm sure that pushed me to become better at everything that I did.

The headlights from the truck were the only source of light within sight as we bounced down the bumpy driveway toward the road. We took a right on Mason Road, then skipped across Wasden Road to the far end of our property. By the time we got to the north end, the sun was starting to rise over the treetops, and I was hoping that it would warm things up. We saw multiple deer along the left side of the road, where I loved to hunt in a big swamp. Dad handed me a piece of jerky and looked over at me with a smirk on his face before saying, "It sure would be a fine morning to be deer hunting." I knew he was joking and rubbing it in, but it was still hard to take my mind off of it.

We finally made it to the old logging road where the two big oak trees had fallen over the crossing into the hayfield. "There they are, boy. That will be enough firewood to get us through the winter." We both hopped out of the truck and grabbed the saws. I was already freezing, but I knew that once we got started, we would warm up quickly.

The old McCullough chainsaws grumbled as they struggled to run, but once they started, the songbirds and hoot owls no longer ruled the morning. The saws screamed out as we worked our way from one end of the tree to the other. Once we got the first tree cut up, we backed Dad's truck up to the bigger pieces and hooked the chains to them. We dragged them out of the way so we could get in to cut up the second tree. Once we finished, we took the wood, load by load, back to the woodshed behind the house so that it could be split up and seasoned for firewood.

I guess Dad forgot about breakfast because we never stopped from start to finish. I was proud to say that we got it done and that we worked together like a fine oiled machine.

The smile on Dad's face and his light-hearted mood suggested that my "punishment" was over and my debt was paid in full, but I was about to find out that there was much more for me to learn from the incident with Will McCrae.

2

THE FORBIDDEN ROOM

That same evening after dinner, Dad called us all to the living room. He tossed wood on the fire, pulled out his Bible, and began to read to us. He read from the Book of Matthew, my favorite chapter of the Bible. Before long, Anna had fallen asleep in Mama's lap as she was gently rubbing her back. There is no way that Dad would have allowed me to fall asleep, but that was fine by me. I loved listening to Dad read the Word of God.

As he was reading, I couldn't help but notice that the scripture aligned with my current situation. He read aloud, "Jesus said, 'Come to me all of you who are weary and burdened and I will give you rest.'" Deep in my heart, I did not know if I had handled the situation on the bus correctly, and it had become a burden to me. I was weary and tired from attempting to work alongside and keep up with my dad. I was just happy to know that I could give all of that to Jesus in prayer and trust that he would help me.

Mama and Anna eventually made their way to my parents' room, leaving Dad and me by the fireplace. Dad added another log to the dying fire and asked me to hang around for a minute. He said, "I appreciate your help today, son. You worked hard. I've got one more thing that I want you to do, though.

"Your grandma needs your help next door. It's time to clean that back room out, and you know that she can't get around like she used to." I didn't hesitate to let him know that I would be glad to help her. After I agreed, Dad punched me on the arm and said, "That's my boy. Now go say your prayers and go to sleep."

The next morning, I awoke to the smell of bacon and eggs. My entire body hurt, and my hands were blistered from holding the chainsaw that weighed as much as I did. Wiping the sleep from my eyes, I walked into the kitchen. Mama said, "You are moving slowly this morning."

I replied, "Yeah, well, Dad tried to kill me yesterday." She laughed and assured me that I would be just fine. Sundays were very special for my family. Nearly every week, we ate a good breakfast and got ready to go to church afterwards.

Later that morning, we loaded up in Daddy's old single cab Chevrolet and struck out for church. Anna sat in Mama's lap, and I sat in the middle, dodging the gear shifter between my legs. The church that we grew up in was only two miles from our home. It was a small church, but a great church with a pastor who was not afraid to share the gospel. It was located halfway between Pintlala and Hope Hull on a large, beautiful lot. When we grew tired of fishing in the creek, we often went to the pond that accompanied the church.

Ironically, that morning the pastor preached from the Book of Matthew. I found it odd that both Dad's and the preacher's words convicted me. After the message was over, I felt like the Lord was trying to tell me something. We all sang, and afterwards we stayed behind to enjoy a home-cooked potluck meal. I always looked forward to those Sunday meals at the church. I think we all did. That Sunday, I left the church feeling like I needed to draw closer to Jesus and trust that he would take my burdens.

Later, I prepared to go hunting, and I asked Dad what stand he thought I should sit in. He quickly and sternly reminded me that I needed to go over to Grandma Louise's house and give her a hand. After I changed out of my hunting clothes, I walked over to her house. As I walked between the two pear trees and up towards the front porch, I could hear her humming a tune. She was in her porch swing, surrounded by her favorite cats, sewing. I never knew how she kept up with those cats, but she had a relationship with each one.

The truth was that Grandma had become very lonely since the death of my grandfather. I never would have known if I had not heard my dad and uncle discussing it. Grandma moved next door after she lost my grandfather, and Dad moved into their house. It was an old wooden cabin that had been on our property for a very long time. It was small, but it was the perfect size for her. She lived there alone with her cats and an old three-legged dog that she had rescued and taken in. She truly was one of a kind and an old-fashioned country lady.

As I walked up her steps, she said, "John, you look more and more like your grandfather every day."

"Yes, ma'am, Dad tells me that all of the time."

She asked me why I was visiting and said, "I figured you would be hunting." I told her that Dad had asked me to come over and help her instead. She smiled and nodded her head, "You are such a good boy to give up your time to come help me. Get over here and sit down beside me."

Her tan hands looked like she had spent her entire life doing manual labor, as if there were deep rivers and streams running through them. She was a quarter Creek Indian, and she was the most peaceful, soft-spoken woman that I knew. She never left our property unless someone came and picked her up for a special trip because she never had a driver's license.

When Grandma needed groceries, my dad or uncle would bring them by. There was also an older gentleman called Sonny from our community who would stop by and visit with her in an attempt to take her out. I think she enjoyed the company, but she never entertained his offers because she missed my grandfather. She always said a part of her heart was buried along with him, and I don't think that she was prepared to go dig it up.

As we slowly rocked back and forth on the swing, she said, "You could have gone hunting. This is more of your dad and uncle's idea than it is mine, but I reckon they are right. It is a mess back there." She told me that when Dad moved her into the old cabin, she put all of my grandfather's things in the back room. "After that, I never opened the door to that room again," she said. Even though it had been fifteen years since my Grandpa had passed, I don't think she could handle the heartbreak. She assured me that it was something that couldn't be done in one day and told me that I could get it done at my own pace.

Growing up, we always stayed in front of Grandma's small cabin. The door at the back of the kitchen was always known to be off limits. My curiosity was aroused when Grandma mentioned my grandfather, so I urged her to come show me what she wanted done. I helped her up off the swing and handed her the walking cane that leaned beside her. As Grandma stood up, she began to cough uncontrollably, but she quickly assured me that she was fine.

I followed her and the old dog we called Tripod inside. Wherever Grandma went, Tripod was not far behind her. He was a blue-tongued mutt that showed up at her house severely injured. His left back leg had been shot off by an angry farmer when he would not stop harassing the farmer's cows. He was only loyal to one person, and that was the old lady who tended to his wounds and saved his life. They were best friends, and though none of us thought the old dog was worth much, we knew he kept Grandma company.

As we walked through the cluttered living room and took a right into the kitchen, she offered me a glass of sweet tea. I was happy to take her up on the offer, and then I went straight for the door that led to the back room. She stopped me before I could reach the door and told me she had to find the key. I had no idea why she would have it locked, but for some reason, she did. After what seemed like an eternity, she returned from her room with the key and unlocked the door.

When the door swung open, all I could see were boxes covered in dust. They started from beside the door and ran the length of both walls and around an old bed. The back door was not visible due to the boxes being stacked so high. I looked back at Grandma when I heard her laughing, and she said, "Boy, you should have seen the size of your eyes when I opened that door!"

I knew it was going to be a tall task, but I would have done anything for her. Deep down, I was honestly excited about being able to feel that close to my grandfather. I had heard so many stories about him, and Dad always talked about how much we had in common. In a way, my hero was a man that I had never met, and I was eager to dive into the dust-covered boxes.

Grandma came in and pulled the curtains open, letting some light into the dusty room. The first things that caught my eye were the traps that lined the top of the walls. It was like stepping back in time. There were old, rusty beaver traps along with some coil spring traps for catching foxes and coyotes. They obviously had not been used in a while because Dad had not run the trap line since Grandpa passed. There for a moment, I got wrapped up in my own emotions and became increasingly curious.

Before I could ask any questions, I noticed that Grandma was getting emotional. She couldn't seem to look at any of it without breaking down. I went over and wrapped my arms around her to comfort her, and she said, "I wish that you could have met him." I knew at that moment just how much she missed her husband and best friend.

After I helped her to the couch, I went back and started digging through the first box. The first things that I saw were a pair of old shoes that were heavily worn down along the outside edges and a Red Man chewing tobacco ball cap. The next box was full of old notebooks and receipts. Grandad started and ran a country store out of an old dance hall when he was a young man. It was located at the end of our dirt road and sat along the side of Mason Road. The store had been closed for the last fifteen years because my dad and uncle were just too busy working their own jobs to keep it open.

As I picked through the receipts and notebooks, I could not help but notice how neat his handwriting was. Most of the receipts were for groceries, gas, and beer. I also read where he had written people's names along with their credit balances. I recognized some of the last names among the pages and figured that Grandpa was doing a lot of favors for his friends and family.

After a couple of hours sorting through the boxes, I hadn't found anything significant. I felt bad for Grandma as I showed her the contents of each box. It was hard watching her react to each sentimental item. Honestly, the thought of throwing his things away made me sick to my stomach, but the truth was that it was taking up too much room and collecting dust. It had been fifteen years, and even though it was painful, it had to be done.

Not long after I came inside to grab another box, I heard Dad come in the front door. As I passed him on the way back out, he asked, "You getting it done, boy?" I stopped and told him that I had cleaned out a trail wide enough to walk to the back of the room. He just laughed and told me to hurry back in so that I could say goodbye to Grandma.

When I came back inside, I didn't see him in the living room, so I walked to the back room. Dad was standing there in the doorway with his hands on his hips, and it seemed like he was soaking in the memories. He said, "It's been a long time since I've seen the inside of this room. It almost feels like he is here with us." After I received a pat on the back and a sad smile from him, we went and told Grandma goodbye. Before we walked out the door, I assured her that I would be back the next day after school.

When we sat down in the truck, Dad told me that my best friend Junior would be riding to school with us the next morning. He said that Junior's dad, Sam, had gotten a new job in Montgomery and that he would be taking us to school for a while. Sam was one of my dad's best friends, and like Junior and me, they had been around each other since birth. Sam was always around, and he was one of the funniest men that I knew. He also worked very hard for everything that he had. Growing up with my dad and working alongside my grandfather during the hot Alabama summers forged a bond among the three of them. Sam was like a brother to my dad and uncle, just like Junior and I were as close as brothers. As far back as anyone knew, the Jones and the Harrison families were tightly knit.

After Dad and I made it back to our house, we washed up and got ready for dinner. Deep down, I was hoping that he would ask me about my time at Grandma's. Fortunately, I knew whatever was on his mind would be shared at the dinner table. When I heard Mama calling my name from the kitchen, I knew that it was time to eat. I jumped up from my bed and ran as hard as I could to the living room. I almost ran into Dad, who was coming out of the kitchen carrying a bowl of biscuits. He said, "Whoa, boy, what did I tell you about running in the house?" I don't think he knew how excited I was to share how my day went with everyone.

When we all sat down for dinner, we asked God to bless the food, just like we always did. Dad wouldn't have been considered a highly educated man, but he sure could talk to the Lord like nobody I had ever heard. I think that is what drew my mother to him and what kept their marriage going. They had their bad days, just like everyone else, but they always worked it out. They both prayed often, and sometimes I would even see them holding hands and praying together.

After Dad made his plate, I barely let him take a bite before I spoke up. "You wouldn't believe all of the things that I found today going through Grandpa's stuff," I said.

"Oh, yeah, what did you find in those old boxes?"

I went on to tell them about the traps, notebooks, receipts, and hats that I had seen. Both Mom and Dad seemed intrigued, but they both lost interest after I went on and on. I seemed to be the only one excited about seeing Grandpa's stuff, and that was fine with me.

After dinner, I was full as a tick and ready to get in bed. Mama called me onto the back porch and handed my school clothes to me. "I did the best that I could to get the blood out of them," she said, giving me a disappointed look. Doing laundry was Mama's time to go outside and be alone. In the backyard, she had a clothesline running from one peach tree to another. She still hand-washed all of our clothes every couple of days and hung them outside to dry.

When I saw the faint blood stains on my jeans, all I could think about was dealing with Will McCrae at school. Surprisingly, we hadn't heard anything about the fight from him or his father. I was hoping that it would all blow over and that everyone would forget about it. Unfortunately, dealing with the McCraes had never been that convenient.

3

X Marks The Spot

The next morning, I awoke to the sound of Junior's dad, Sam, laughing on the front porch. I walked down the hall, through the living room, and out the front door. Sam said, "Good morning, young man. I heard you had to handle some business on the school bus on Friday."

After I told him about what happened, he said, "Yeah, Junior said you roughed him up pretty good. Looks like you have the same fighting side that your granddad had." While I was doing my best to listen to Sam, I was thinking that if Junior had already heard about the fight, then word must be traveling fast.

Dad and Sam continued to talk on the porch while I went inside to get dressed. I was putting my boots on when I heard a truck coming down the driveway. I figured it was my uncle coming by to talk with Dad and Sam, but my heart dropped when I walked outside and saw the truck. It was a brand new Ford truck that looked like it had never seen a mud hole. My heart seemed like it was going to jump out of my chest when I saw Billy McCrae step out and head our way.

"Good morning," Billy said.

Dad replied, "Morning, what brings you through here so early, Billy?"

"Oh, I think you know why I am here unless your boy has not told you the truth about what happened on the school bus Friday." I could tell that things were about to go sour when Dad stood up out of his rocking chair.

"Yeah, John told me about how your son was picking on my daughter Anna."

"Oh, is that all he told you?" Billy asked.

Dad quickly responded, "No, he told me William called him a coward, which looks to be false based on that black eye I see on William's face, but you already know that there are no cowards around here."

Billy's face began to turn red, and we could tell that he had a lot to say. Billy was arrogant, but he wasn't ignorant, and I think he realized that he was in the wrong place to say the wrong thing.

I could see William in the truck, urging his father to get back in the driver's seat. Before Billy sat down, he stopped and looked back at Dad, "You better teach that boy of yours some manners before something bad happens to him."

Dad rushed off the porch and toward Billy, but Sam stopped him and said, "Henry, stop. It ain't worth it!" Sam turned, looked at Billy, "You better get on out of here, Billy, before something bad happens to you."

I had only seen my father lose his temper a few times. Each time was quite spread out, and each time was quite scary. That morning, he was awfully close to making a mistake. I had heard Mama talk about him having a mean streak that he had buried down deep. I was thinking Billy McCrae better be glad Jesus had gotten a hold of my old man.

Billy sped down the driveway, slinging rocks and leaving in a cloud of dust. Sam called Junior up on the porch, and he and Dad sat us down together. Sam said, "Y'all need to steer clear of that boy at school, ya hear. He is just like his old man, and our families have never agreed on much. There is some bad blood there, and we ain't digging up the past. I've got to get to work, but y'all have a good day at school. Junior, I'll pick you up here after work."

I became curious when Sam mentioned digging up the past, so I asked Dad what he was talking about. He assured me that one day he would tell me, but he was still visibly angry as he was driving us to school. My father was never one to open up about his past, and that always puzzled me. So we rode toward Pintlala with nothing but the sound of the old mud grip tires to drown out the silence.

As we pulled up to Pintlala school and parked, Dad said, "Y'all remember what we talked about this morning now." Then, when we got out of the truck and made our way toward the classroom, I noticed everybody staring at us. I did not want a bad reputation at school, but I was afraid that because of who I had fought, the truth would get twisted. One thing that I was sure of was that William and his friends would be barking up the wrong tree if they caught Junior and me together. Junior always had my back, and I always had his.

Junior and I were raised on farms right down the road from each other. I was of average height, but I was stout like all of the other men in our family. Junior was tall for a fourteen-year-old and was definitely built like Sam, tall and muscular. The troublemakers at school never gave him a hard time, and I am not sure if it was because they knew Junior was tough or if it was because he was one of the few colored students in our school.

Our school was predominantly white, and just like any other place, there were some bad apples. The McCrae family was among those who were racist, and that was obvious. I always wondered how people like the McCrae family were so respected when they were far from deserving that respect.

I never saw color because I was raised to treat everyone the same. My best friend was colored, and my father's best friend was colored. It just was not in me to judge someone based on the color of their skin. We played together, we worked together, and we didn't listen to the people who disagreed. We all knew that they didn't understand.

After we made it to class and settled in for the day, I began to daydream about being back at Grandma's house. I was excited that Junior would be at the house after school because he could help me go through the boxes. The day crept by slowly, and other than everyone staring and whispering behind our backs, Junior, Anna and I all had a normal day.

After school, we made our way outside to the old bus that stayed parked under the massive pine trees. I knew William would have his crew with him, but when I looked over at Junior walking beside me, I felt relieved. When Miss Bibb saw us, she opened the door to the bus and told us to load up. I figured it would be wise for the three of us to sit right behind her. William and his crew would go to the back of the bus, so when they walked past us, Miss Bibb would be able to hear what they said. I had it planned out from thinking about it in class all day.

William was one of the last people to get on the bus behind his friends. Other than a long, awkward stare down when he walked by us, nothing happened. It was hard not to feel some pride when I saw him walk by me with a nasty black eye. I don't think I was proud of what I had done, but I was proud to know that I was capable of protecting my family.

After we turned onto our road, I told Miss Bibb that she could drop us off in front of Grandma's house. When we unloaded, I told Anna to go home and tell my mother that Junior and I were helping Grandma. My grandma loved Junior just like she loved his father, Sam. She had practically raised Sam alongside her own children, so she was happy to see us when we knocked on the door.

Grandma came to the door to open it while telling Tripod to "shut up and quit barking." He was a protective old rascal, but he was usually fine once he came up and smelled you for a minute. Junior wasn't too fond of Tripod, and I could see why. He was used to being around well-trained coon dogs, and he didn't see much value in a grumpy old mutt.

Of course, Grandma offered us a glass of sweet tea when we got inside. I wasn't thirsty, but since she kept the cabin around eighty degrees year round, I took her up on the offer. I never liked to tell her no because I knew she looked forward to asking me. After Junior and I talked with Grandma and finished our tea, we made our way into the dusty old bedroom.

Junior was blown away by how many boxes were still left in the room. Grandma said, "Y'all get busy and let me know if you need anything." We started on the right hand side of the room and figured we could make it at least to the foot of the old bed. I could tell Junior wasn't too excited about cleaning up, but personally, I couldn't wait to see what was in the boxes.

The first few boxes were old clothes, shoes and hats. The next row of boxes we came to was heavy and obviously did not have clothes in them. Once we started to open the boxes, I realized they were full of tools that my grandpa used on his trap line. I knew Dad would want to keep those boxes and put them in our barn, so we set them aside. We also put all of his old traps that were lining the top of the walls in the same boxes.

Afterward, we made our way closer to the foot of the bed, where three dusty boxes remained. It felt good to know we had almost half of the room cleaned out. When I opened the first of the three boxes, my heart jumped. I saw old shotgun shells, turkey calls, and layers of turkey feathers.

I hadn't felt excitement like this since I started cleaning the room out. It was something that my Grandfather and I had in common. I loved to turkey hunt and only started turkey hunting because of the stories that I had heard about him. I could not wait to see what was in the other two boxes.

One of the last two boxes was full of turkey beards and spurs. These were kept by my Grandfather to remind him of how special each different turkey was. After being harvested, they were taken off of the Tom to be respected and appreciated by whatever hunter saw them. In a way, they were like a trophy, but so much more.

The third box had a set of rattling antlers tied together with orange hay baling twine. Also among the things that caught my attention were rifle cartridges, an old trumpet turkey call, and a small leather book. I immediately grabbed the trumpet call and started using it to make a familiar sound. Junior and I looked at each other and smiled because he knew that I would be attempting to master that call until the next spring.

I noticed Junior staring behind me, so I spun around back towards the door. Grandma was in the doorway with a smile on her face. She said, "I haven't heard that turkey call in probably twenty years. Your grandfather used to drive me nuts with that thing. I left him alone when I figured out he wasn't going to stop." That was just confirmation for me that I had a new favorite turkey call.

After Grandma walked out, Junior handed me a small piece of paper that was rolled up like a scroll. He said that it had fallen out of the trumpet call when I lifted it from the box. We looked at each other in confusion. I did not think much about it to be honest, but I am glad that Junior was curious.

Junior asked, "Well, are you going to read it?"

"It's probably just trash," I said. Boy, I was sorely mistaken. The first words that I could see as I unrolled the paper matched the handwriting from Grandpa's receipt notebooks.

I looked at Junior and said, "This is a handwritten letter from my Grandpa, Junior." Why was a note rolled up and hidden in his favorite turkey call?

He had beautiful cursive handwriting, and I felt blessed to be able to read it. The letter read, "If you are reading this, then I know you are family. The real family treasure lies in the Magnolia Hole. X marks the spot." Then we saw at the bottom of the page where he had signed his name and dated it.

"Can you believe this?" I asked Junior.

Junior replied, "Where is the Magnolia Hole, and what is he talking about?"

I said, "I have no idea, but we need to find out." We sat there on the floor for a few minutes in silence, staring at the letter with both of our imaginations running wild.

I then realized that we had not yet opened the small leather book that was packed with the turkey call. I reached into the box for the dusty book, not knowing that opening it would change my life forever. As I opened it, I realized just how old and frail the book was.

Among the first pages were lists of the fur-bearing animals that he had trapped. On each page, he had recorded the date, animal, and location of the trap. He then wrote the price of what each fur sold for. I got lost in history and amazement as I read that small book.

When I reached the last few pages of the book, I found a loose piece of paper that had been folded. When I unfolded the fragile paper, I could see a map. The map had been drawn by hand with a pencil. It was also signed and dated just like the note from the turkey call.

I could see the creek at the top of the map, but that was all I could make out. It was almost sunset, so we didn't have enough light in the room to study the map. I decided that I would call it an evening and read it later at home. We had put in a solid two hours of work and had everything on the right side of the room cleaned out.

After Junior and I said goodbye to Grandma, we hurried off the front porch and down the driveway. I pulled the map from my pocket and told Junior I was going to show my father. Junior said, "What if he goes and finds it before we do?" Then I assured him Dad would decipher the map without knowing what was going on.

Sam pulled down the driveway not too long after Junior and I made it back home. Mom invited Sam in for dinner, but he declined her offer. He said that Georgia Lee would have dinner waiting on the table for them. When Sam told Junior to load up, Junior leaned over and quietly said, "Don't forget to show your dad the map."

That night, Dad came home later than usual. We had already finished dinner and gotten washed up for the night by the time he walked inside. He was dirty and tired, but I knew I had to find time to ask him about the map. I knew it might be my only opportunity to ask when he sat down and asked Mama if there were any leftovers from dinner.

Dad bent over to take his boots off, and I snuck up beside him. I began to unfold the map without saying anything, and I made sure to crinkle the paper as loudly as I could to spark his curiosity. After he took his boots off, he turned and asked, "What is that?" I couldn't wait to show him because finding the family treasure depended on his ability to decipher the map.

After I had his full attention, I told him it was a map that Junior and I had found going through Grandpa's things. Dad asked, "What sort of map? What does it say?" I slowly slid the map across the table, and he quickly took it from me. He studied the map in silence for a few minutes and handed it back to me. My heart dropped when I thought he wasn't going to say anything.

A few moments later, he broke the silence and said, "I've never seen that map, but it is a spot that your Grandpa used to set beaver traps. I don't know why he would have drawn a map of it, but it is called the Magnolia Hole." I couldn't believe it! I knew when I saw Grandpa had signed and dated both the letter and the map that the two were linked.

I was trying to hide my excitement when Dad asked, "Where did you find that map and what are you going to do with it?" I told him that I was just curious about the map and why Grandpa would have drawn it. He replied, "Well, I don't know. Maybe that X he drew by the big oak is where he set his beaver traps."

I could barely contain myself when I realized that Dad knew exactly where Grandpa was talking about. I had to find out where it was without being too obvious. "So you've seen the big oak that he marked on the map?" I asked.

"Oh, yeah, it is right by the creek. I grew up down there helping your Grandpa run his trap line," he replied.

I wanted to be more discreet, but I couldn't help myself, so I asked him if he could show me where it was. He said, "After school tomorrow, you and Junior meet me at the hay barn. I've been out there trying to fix the storm damage from this past summer. It's not far from the barn, so I can point you in the right direction." I didn't know if he was being serious or just trying to recruit us to help him work on the barn. That was a risk that we would have to take because finding the Magnolia Hole would put us one step closer to finding the family treasure.

4

The Magnolia Hole

The next day at school, I was useless because I was only focused on one thing. I felt like I was hiding a secret, but I didn't even know what the secret was. All day, Junior and I talked about it as much as we could without anyone hearing us. He was just as excited as I was, and if anyone could be a part of it, I was glad it was him.

I felt like I had been in a rut and my mind was fogged by the things that had been going on. I had been so worried about William McCrae and his father. I was only thinking about the fight and wondering if I had done the right thing. I knew everyone was talking about it, and I didn't like being the center of attention. Finding the letter and map from Grandpa was taking my mind off the things that had been weighing me down. It gave me purpose and direction.

I was focused on what had to be done, but the weight of the responsibility was heavy. Because of the way it had happened, I couldn't help but think that I was meant to find that letter and map. Finding the family treasure was going to be up to me, and I was just hoping that I would be cut out for the job. With all of the thoughts that were running through my head, it was almost as if this was my destiny.

Everyone has a calling on their life, and I was anxious to see if this was mine. The whole situation had felt like a dream so far, but maybe that was because I wasn't the one pulling the strings. Maybe finding the map and the family treasure was all part of God's plan. I thought to myself, "Surely, this is God answering my prayers."

After Junior, Anna and I got off the bus that afternoon, we walked down the driveway toward the house. From a distance, I could see Mama walking across the porch and into the house. I let Anna get ahead of us so that she couldn't hear what Junior and I were saying. Then Junior and I devised a plan before we went inside to talk to Mama.

I found her pulling meat from the ice box and told her that Dad had asked us to meet him at the hay barn. She agreed to let us go, but told me to be back in time for dinner, even if we had to walk home. There was no way that I was allowing Dad to miss dinner again because the barn was half a mile from the house. I think that was Mama's way of telling me to drag Dad's butt home in time for dinner.

After Mama gave us permission to leave, we walked out of the back door and toward the old horse barn. I told Junior, "There is a shovel in the last horse stall on the left."

"Okay," he said. "I'll grab it while you keep watch." I stood at the entrance of the barn watching Mama through the window. When I saw her walk out of the kitchen, I bolted around the corner of the barn and met Junior.

Instead of taking the driveway to the road, we cut through the woods behind the house. I didn't want Mama to see the shovel and wonder what we were up to. I told Junior how far it was to the hay barn, but he didn't seem worried at all. We had a good walk ahead of us.

After we snuck into the woods behind the house, we turned left and followed an old trail towards the main road. Once we came to the road, we followed it down toward the north end of our property. We stayed just inside the tree line to avoid any prying eyes, and passed the time by discussing what we would do if we actually found the treasure.

"What if it is all gold or diamonds?" Junior asked.

"I don't think Grandpa would have liked to see his family work so hard if he had that kind of money hidden away. He did say it was treasure in his letter, though." I was thinking, "What could have possibly been hidden there for all of these years?" It was a mystery to me and Junior, but it was a mystery that we were set on solving.

Once we reached the intersection of Mason and Wasden roads, we quickly slipped across. We disappeared into the woods and navigated around the low spots that held water. For the most part, our property was a large creek bottom, but we had multiple fields on the higher ground. Dad would often plant peas and corn in the fertile sloughs, but he saved the pastures for the hay.

As we closed the distance, I could hear the sound of a hammer beating against wood. I warned Junior that we were getting close and that we needed to hide the shovel. Separating the fields was a small tree line and a narrow stream. We both agreed that it was the perfect spot to leave the shovel, so we propped it up against a white oak and left it there.

We skipped across the stream and into the next field. The noise from the hammer was getting much closer. As we came to the top of the rise, we were both relieved to finally see the old barn in the distance. On the opposite side of the field, Dad began to wave at us and climb down the ladder.

The previous summer, a bad storm produced hail and straight-line winds that put the barn to the test. Dad had been putting it off, but I guess he finally decided to patch it up. He kept some of our hay from the north end under the barn that had been built before he was born. We would also park equipment there out of the weather. So even though it was old, the barn served its purpose.

Dad came out to meet us and said, "I'm surprised that you showed up. I ought to make both of you help me finish up." He then laughed and said, "No, I'm not going to make you boys work this afternoon. Walk down to the edge of the woods with me." Junior and I fell in behind him and followed him down to the tree line.

He pointed down into the bottom and said, "I'm going to show you the fastest way, but it may not be the easiest way. Cross that ditch and walk until you come to a thicket. Once you make it through the thicket, you will come to an opening and a bend in the creek. When you see that bend in the creek, you know that you have reached the Magnolia Hole. The big oak on the map will be on this side of the creek."

I said, "Oh, I was down there deer hunting last year."

"No, I don't think you went that far," Dad replied. Then he told us to keep our eyes open for cottonmouths, and we were on our way.

We made our way to the bottom, and I told Junior that one of us needed to circle back around and get the shovel. He said that he would stay there, and I agreed since I knew the lay of the land. So I snuck through the bottom and up over the ridge past the barn. I felt bad for sneaking around on Dad, but I knew he would understand if I found the treasure.

I found the shovel by the big White Oak and made my way back toward Junior. I could hear Dad hammering away again, so that helped calm my nerves. I could not help but notice the amount of deer sign that I was seeing. I had hunted in that area the last couple of years, but it hadn't paid off yet. Dad and I normally hunted from the ground, but I couldn't help thinking about how good a spot it would be for a tree stand.

After I walked down the ridge and back over the top, I saw Junior's blue shirt in the distance. Once I dropped down into the bottom with him, I could see him plain as day. I was sure that Dad hadn't seen me circle around, but Junior was still nervous. Maybe he was just as anxious as I was to sink that shovel into the dirt.

We made our way down the hill and to the steep ditch at the bottom. It was too wide to jump across, so we had no choice but to get dirty. We walked parallel to the ditch until we found a well-established deer crossing. It was much cleaner, and the last thing we wanted to do was get bitten by a snake that we couldn't see.

I started down the steep side of the ditch with Junior coming down behind me. The slippery mud gave way under our feet, and we both slid to the bottom. It wasn't the most efficient way down, but it was definitely the fastest way. We both looked at each other and laughed, then began dusting the sand off our pants.

When I stood up, I could see the massive deer trail going up the other side. Their hooves had made deep holes in the soft mud as they attempted to climb out of the deep ditch. I knew it wasn't going to be possible for us to climb, so I came up with an idea. There was no way I was yelling for Dad to come pull us out of the ditch.

The ditch led back to the main creek, so we could just walk the ditch and follow it down. As we slowly walked in that direction, I began to get an eerie feeling. It was getting narrow, and we both knew that we were in snake country. We hadn't made it very far when Junior said, "Look at that tree. We can climb out there." Sure enough, there was a tree hanging down over the ditch.

For some reason, the tree was deformed, and it grew horizontally before it straightened out. It made a ninety-degree angle and a perfect place to escape the ditch. Both Junior and I jumped up, grabbed the tree, and easily pulled ourselves out. The first thing we noticed was the wall of dense underbrush in front of us. "This is the thicket that dad was talking about," I said.

Junior laughed, "So, I guess that means we have to go through it."

"Come on, let's go. It will be worth it," I said.

Everything was designed to hold us back and slow us down. The sharp briars were grabbing us below the waist, and the vines were twisting around us. I could feel the briars penetrating my jeans as I struggled forward. Every five feet, we stopped and pulled ourselves free. It made for a long, rough journey through the thicket.

As we neared the other side of the thicket, I saw daylight shining in an opening. I told Junior, "That's the Magnolia Hole. We are almost there." I think the mosquitoes carried us the rest of the way, and we made it to the opening. Junior and I looked at each other, and we both asked the same thing at the same time, "Where is the big oak?"

We made our way through the opening, and I began to study our surroundings. Junior stopped in front of me and said, "Which one is it going to be? They are all big oaks."

I replied, "We need to push in further towards the creek." I remembered when Dad said that the big oak was on our side of the creek, so it would be hard to miss.

We skipped down the sandy embankment and off the back side of the Magnolia Hole. After we made it through the sugar cane, we came to the edge of Pintlala Creek. I found a spot in the shade, sat on a washed up log, and took a break. Junior smiled when I pulled the map from my back pocket and began to study it. He asked, "Are we getting any closer? What does the map say?"

I stood up and answered, "We need to keep going until we come to a deep turn in the creek, and it should be there."

We had walked a couple of hundred yards before I saw the creek starting to turn left. When we had made it a little further, I told Junior that it looked like the creek was coming to a dead end. In fact, the creek turned left at such a sharp angle, it only appeared as a dead end. I looked up and noticed massive limbs stretching out over the creek. The sunlight was blinding me as I attempted to follow one massive limb to its source.

"Uh, Junior, I think we found our tree," I said. We both followed the long, sweeping limbs back to the base of the tree, but realized that we could not see it. The creek bank was so steep that it served as a wall blocking our view. Smirking, I looked at Junior, "Well, there is only one way up."

We dug the toes of our boots into the sandy bank and used the vines to climb to the top. Once we both made it to the top and caught our breath, I heard Junior say, "Oh, my gosh. "The ancient, gigantic oak tree was sitting in an opening all by itself. It was as if the thick woods around it were not allowed to come any closer. We would have had to be legally blind to miss it.

The tree was at least six to eight feet across at the base. Junior and I spread our arms out, side by side, and we couldn't reach a third of the way around the tree. It looked to have been as big around as a full-sized pickup truck at the base. I had seen some huge oak trees, but I had never seen one half the size of this one. Junior and I figured that the tree had to be hundreds of years old.

We studied the map for a brief time and found the direction in which we should be searching for the X. When we walked around the other side of the tree, we saw a low spot in the ground. It was twenty yards from the base of the tree, and it stuck out like a sore thumb. When Junior and I walked over and studied the low area, we knew that we had possibly found the spot.

Normally, people do not want their treasure discovered when they hide it, but it seemed as if my grandpa wanted this to be found. He had known that whoever found that note and map would be family, and he probably figured that if someone had come in as far as the Magnolia Hole to find it, they deserved it. That is what I was telling myself anyway.

Junior and I drew straws to see who would dig first, and it came down to me. I didn't mind at all because I was eager to see what was buried beneath the surface. Each time the shovel struck the dirt, we knew we were closer. It had all lined up too well for us to be off the mark.

The ground was surprisingly soft, and thankfully, I did not hit any tree roots. I dug a couple of feet down and then out of breath, passed the shovel to Junior. He gladly stepped in and got to work. Junior began attacking the hole like he was mad at it. I could tell it wasn't his first time using a shovel.

We became disappointed after a while. Junior had dug down to three feet, and we still didn't have anything. Junior sat down beside the hole and passed the shovel back to me. Neither one of us wanted to admit it, but it was possible that we had chosen the wrong spot.

I stepped up to the hole and decided that I would give it one more try. I dug down to four feet, and out of nowhere, my shovel hit something solid. Junior came alive and said, "You hit something; it sounded like wood."

"Yeah, I bet it is a big root. It's probably nothing."

With each scoop of dirt that came out of the hole, it was becoming increasingly obvious that it was not a root. Junior joined me, and from opposite sides of the hole, we began to dig by hand. Before too long, I started to see square corners and straight edges. I asked, "Man, are you seeing what I am seeing?" and Junior replied, "We actually found it."

Finally, I saw a wooden chest lying before us. We worked the tight dirt around the outsides of the chest to free it up. Once we got it loose, I knew I had to use my shovel to get under the chest and lift it out of the hole. It had to weigh a ton if it was full of gold and diamonds.

Just as I was getting ready to get under the case with the shovel, Junior reached down and pulled it out by hand. I was surprised to see him do that, but even more surprised when he said that it was light as a feather. He said, "Well, it's definitely not full of gold."

I replied, "I assumed it would be heavy, but I guess I was wrong." I began to wonder if we had dug up an empty chest.

We both hit our knees in the shade that the massive oak provided. We took our pocket knives and began to chip away at the mud on the chest. It was around eighteen inches long and twelve inches tall. The area on the front was caked with mud so badly that we couldn't tell if it was locked or not. Once we cleaned the front, we saw that it had a latch, but it wasn't locked.

Afterward, I quickly stood up and grabbed the shovel. Junior said, "You are going to break that chest if you hit it with the shovel."

"We can't carry the chest out of here anyway. Nobody else can see it. We've got to see what is inside before we leave," I said. He agreed and stood back at a safe distance.

I set the chest down in a clean, open spot away from dirt and the hole. First, I attempted to stab downward at the latch. We were hoping it would break easily so that we would not damage the chest. After I had hit it five times, the latch had not budged. We attempted to free it up with our knives again, but we had no luck.

Frustrated, I decided to hit it as hard as I could and try to get lucky. We saw sparks fly as the metal shovel met the latch. Fortunately, the latch was broken and the chest had not been damaged. Junior joked, "Remind me not to make you mad while you have a shovel in your hands."

We then stared at each other in a moment of silence. I could barely catch my breath, and my heart was pounding in my chest. Junior was staring back at me and waiting for me to give the order. I could not believe that we were actually standing over something Grandad had buried years before. I had no idea how the contents of the chest would change my life forever.

5

A Hiding Place

Junior and I slipped our pocket knife blades through the cracks on both ends of the chest. I counted to three, and we popped it open. Before I could say a word, Junior asked, "What is that?" Some sort of neatly folded animal pelt sat before us at the bottom of the chest. "Is it alive?"

Laughing, I pulled it out and began to carefully unfold the pelt. What we found inside was an old leather book similar to the one that we found at Grandma's house. Junior became frustrated and said, "Man, we just did all of that work for a dang book." Disappointed, I set the book down on the top of the chest and walked away.

Unfortunately, there was no money, gold, or anything else that would make us all rich. Why had we gotten our hopes up? I began to feel foolish and disgusted at the same time. All of a sudden, it seemed like we were no longer running on adrenaline. It began to feel like a failed mission.

After we stepped away and complained for a few minutes, I started to think that it may be an old Bible. I stared at the book sitting on top of the chest as I attempted to find something to be positive about. Surprisingly, the book was in good condition after being underground for so long. It favored a journal more than a Bible, and it was obviously very old.

"Well, are you going to open it up or not?" Junior asked. "We may as well see what we just risked our necks for."

We walked over, and I carefully opened the book to the first page. I immediately recognized the handwriting. It read, "This is an eyewitness account of the events that took place on this property in 1865 and the years after. This journal holds the true story and our family treasure." Below that, at the bottom of the page, it was signed, "Pat Harrison -1904."

My mind was racing as I tried to figure out how the book was considered to be a treasure. Junior was pacing around the clearing while shaking his head and mumbling to himself. So much had happened so fast, and I was struggling to wrap my head around it all. How had we been so naive to think that we were actually going to find real treasure buried in the woods?

The truth was that we had gotten our hopes up and been let down. The only positive thing I could think of was that we had actually found what we were looking for. There had to be a reason that Pat went out of his way to create this mystery. If there was a real reason, Junior and I were far from knowing what it was.

After Junior made his way back over to me, he asked, "Why would your grandpa bury a book in the middle of the dang woods?"

"Your guess is as good as mine. Maybe there was a secret that he had been protecting for all of these years", I replied. "There has to be something that we are missing."

Out of curiosity, I began to skim through the journal from the front to the back. It was the only way to know if our adventure had been a complete waste of time or not. Pat's handwriting covered the pages from the first to the last. He had a story to tell, and for some reason, it was worth burying it in the ground to keep it hidden. My frustration became curiosity, and I began to think about what may be written in the journal.

"These mosquitoes are killing me, man," Junior said loudly. I snapped back into reality and realized that the sun was going down. My mind had been so wrapped up in our situation that I had lost track of time. I remembered that Mama had told me to be home in time for dinner.

I stood up from where I was kneeling and said, "Alright, let's fill in this hole and head back to the barn."

"But what are you going to do with the book and the chest?" Junior asked.

"I am going to take the book with us, and we can leave the chest out here." Suddenly, I felt rushed because the time we spent in the woods had flown by.

I quickly handed the book to Junior and grabbed the shovel. I folded the beaver pelt and placed it back in the chest. My mind was racing so fast that I didn't know what to do, so I just tossed the chest in the hole and began to cover it up. The last thing I needed was for Dad or anyone else to find it, so burying it seemed like the best option.

After I filled the hole, Junior and I kicked leaves over the fresh dirt and tossed some sticks on top. I ran down to the creek and splashed some water on my face to wash away the dirt. I didn't need Mama asking any questions when I got home, so I covered my tracks. I already felt guilty about hiding the fact that we were looking for treasure, but now I really had something to hide.

It wasn't that I did not want to include my family in the important discovery. Selfishly, I wanted to be the first to read it. It was just old-fashioned curiosity and impatience. I felt like it was my calling and destiny to know what was hidden. I had every intention of handing the journal over to Dad when I finished reading it.

Since we were running short on time, we decided to go around the thicket and ditch on the way back to the barn. We followed the winding creek around until I could hear Dad up on the hill. I could tell that he wasn't alone as he carried on a conversation with someone. As we got closer, we realized that it was Sam.

Before we started up the ridge to the edge of the field, Junior grabbed my shoulder and stopped me. He handed me the journal and asked, "Where are you going to hide it? You still have to ride home with Mr. Henry."

"I haven't thought about it yet, but I guess I can slip it behind my belt and let my shirt cover it up." So, I carefully placed the journal between my belt and my back, and we started up the hill.

We made our way into the field, and I could see Sam up on the ladder and Dad sitting on his tailgate. I guess Dad needed a break, and Sam was never one to not step up and help out. Somehow, we closed the distance before they even knew we were coming. The closer we got, the more worried I became that the journal would be visible under my shirt.

"Well, what do we have here?" Sam asked.

"They went on a wild goose chase to the Magnolia Hole for some reason," Dad replied.

"Is that where my old man and Pat pulled that big catfish out of the creek that summer?"

Dad smiled, "Yep, that's the spot."

They went on to tell Junior and me the story behind the record-breaking catfish that our grandfathers had caught in the Magnolia Hole. They also told us how the Magnolia Hole got its name. They said a huge Magnolia tree had fallen, and the root system of the tree had created a deep hole in the shallow creek. The day that Pat and Joe caught the catfish, they named it the Magnolia Hole.

"That is enough for me today, Sam. Sarah is going to tan our hides if John and I aren't on time for supper," Dad said. I let out a sigh of relief because I knew that I wouldn't have to drag him home and away from his work.

"Yeah, Junior and I need to be on our way, too. We will see y'all tomorrow morning."

Junior gave me a look that suggested he was worried about me sneaking around with the journal. I just nodded my head and said, "I'll see you tomorrow morning, Junior."

Then Dad and I loaded up in the truck and followed Sam and Junior out to the gate and the main road. I knew it was risky riding with Dad in his single-cab truck, but he seemed oblivious. I thought to myself, "Calm down, John. He doesn't have a clue."

As we crept down the driveway, I finally began to relax. Sunset was my favorite time of the day. We had the windows rolled down, and the cool air hitting me in the face brought me comfort. The sound of the brown thrashers in the trees alongside the road made me wish I were in the woods hunting. Dad always told me when they started making a racket, the deer were about to move.

Christmas break was coming up, so I would have plenty of time to spend in the woods in the near future. With everything going on in my life, I was beginning to miss the peace and solitude that hunting provided. Life had been hectic, and I needed a break from all of the commotion. I would also need a quiet escape to read the journal, and the base of a tree would make a fine place to do it.

As we passed Grandma's cabin, I couldn't help but think about how this had all started. I wanted to run up to her front porch, knock on the door, and tell her all about the journal. At that time, I knew that was not an option. I knew that she missed Grandpa Pat, and I didn't want to make it any worse. There was also a chance that she would tell my dad or uncle about the journal, and that was not a risk that I was willing to take.

My mother and Anna were sitting on the front porch swing when Dad and I pulled up to the house. I was thinking of a place to hide the journal, and I knew that I had to come up with something quickly. My only two options were the barn out back and my room. Mama cleaned and reorganized my room often, so that meant the barn would be the safer of the two places.

I waited for Dad to get out of the truck so that he wouldn't see the journal if I hopped out first. As soon as he shut the door, I jumped out and quickly slipped the journal under his truck seat. I planned to wait until everyone was asleep so I could sneak out to the barn and hide it in a better place. There was a spot in the corner of the last horse stall that would be perfect.

As Dad and I came up on the porch, Mama said, "Well, I'm surprised, Henry. I thought for sure Anna and I would be eating dinner alone tonight."

Dad laughed, "Sarah, I love your cooking, but sometimes work can't wait. It's a good thing I'm in no rush to finish the roof on that old barn." Mama smiled as Dad walked over and greeted her and Anna with a hug and a kiss.

"John, go inside and get washed up for dinner. How did your clothes get so filthy?" Mama asked. I told her that Junior and I had fallen in the ditch down below the barn. I wasn't lying to her, but I guess I wasn't telling her the whole truth either. Fortunately, she did not question me any further, and I was able to go inside and prepare dinner.

For a while, there was an awkward silence around the dinner table. I had so much on my mind, and I was nervous about sneaking out after bedtime to hide the journal. Mama asked me why I was so quiet, and when

I told her that I had a lot on my mind, she and Dad both began to laugh. She asked, "What in the world does a healthy fourteen-year-old boy have to worry about?"

I replied, "I don't know, Mama. Maybe your cooking is so good that I just don't have much to say."

"John, I was born, but I wasn't born yesterday. When you feel like talking about whatever is on your mind, you just let me know," she said. I agreed to do so, and after I finished my meal, I asked to be excused from the table. Anna was usually the first to lie down, but I figured the earlier that I went to bed, the earlier everyone else might go to bed.

I made my way to my room and climbed into bed. I planned to lie there in the darkness until I heard everyone else go to bed. I could hear Dad stoking the fire and Mama in the kitchen. The sound of Anna running across the hardwood floors seemed to shake the entire house. I was growing impatient as I thought about diving into Pat's journal and reading about something that was obviously very important to him.

Hours later, I awoke to the sound of coyotes howling in the distance. The house was completely silent. I didn't hear anyone stirring around, and I knew that it was time to make my move. I was angry at myself for falling asleep, and I knew that it probably wouldn't be long before the sun came up.

I quietly slipped out of bed and grabbed the flashlight from my bedside table. Knowing that it would be hard to sneak across the hardwood floors, I tiptoed to my bedroom door. Slowly, I eased the door open and made my way down the hallway. When I reached my parents' room, I stopped to listen and make sure they weren't awake. The fire in their room had died down, but I could see well enough to know they were both sound asleep.

Nervously, I closed the distance between their room and the living room. I carried my boots from the front door to the back door and slipped them on. The old screen door always made a loud creaking noise, so I took my time. I slowly opened it just enough to sneak through. Once I made it outside and onto the porch, my anxiety took a backseat to the excitement that I felt.

I turned the flashlight on and walked around to the front of the house. When I got to Dad's truck, I opened the passenger door and grabbed the journal from underneath the seat. Then I made my way to the barn and grabbed one of Dad's hammers that was hanging on a nail. It was so cold that I could see my breath as I hurried towards the last stall on the left.

I pulled the old wooden gate open and walked to the back corner of the stall. Holding the flashlight with my mouth, I used the hammer to pry the bottom board back. I carefully placed the journal in the opening and stuffed hay around it. I had planned on reading the first few pages, but it was too cold and I was ready to get back inside. I then tacked the small nail back in through the board, closing up the hole.

The wooden steps creaked as I made my way up onto the back porch. I took my boots off so that I could walk quietly across the floor inside, successfully slipped inside without the screen door making any noise, and put my boots back where I had found them. The only thing left for me to do was walk down the hallway and into my room.

I was sneaking past my parents' room when I saw a shadow move across the floor. My heart went into my throat when I heard Dad ask, "Son, what are you doing?" He walked out of the darkness and towards me in the doorway.

I said, "The coyotes woke me up, and I had to go to the outhouse."

He jokingly asked, "Well, did you at least warm the seat up for me?"

"No, sir, it was a false alarm."

He walked down the hall and into the darkness, saying, "Go get your butt back in bed."

I climbed into my bed and pulled the warm blankets over my head. My entire body was numb from going outside in nothing but my thin night clothes. The warmth of the blankets provided peace, and I was thankful that Dad hadn't caught me out in the barn. I snuggled in as my mind was racing about the next time that I could put my hands on the journal. It would most likely be Christmas break before I would have the opportunity to do so.

6

LITTLE BROWN JUG

The next morning, Dad shook me and said, "Wake up, boy. You need to go chop firewood before school. Sam and Junior are about to be here." I went to the barn and got the wood maul, but before coming out, I couldn't help myself; I had to look over at the spot where I had hidden the journal. I rested my chin on the cold wooden gate and stared over at the board in the corner. It was a good hiding spot, and in a way, I was proud of myself for successfully sneaking out the night before. I hoped that time would fly by so I could take the journal to the woods with me over Christmas break.

As I was finishing up at the wood pile, I saw Sam's truck coming down the driveway. I dropped the maul and ran around the corner of the house. Junior was already headed my way, and Sam went inside to talk to Dad. Junior quietly asked, "Where is the book? Where did you hide it? "

I grabbed the maul from beside the woodpile and told him to follow me. I took him down to the last stall and showed him where I had hidden the journal. He was impressed with the hiding spot and confirmed what I had already been thinking, "Nobody would ever find it right there."

I noticed that I had forgotten to put Dad's hammer away, so I placed it back on the nail where it had been hanging. Laughing and joking, we made our way back to the front yard and waited for Dad and Sam to come outside.

A few minutes later, Sam came out with a biscuit in his hand and said, "Boy, you sure are lucky your mama is such a good cook."

I smiled, "Yes sir, I know it." Sam jokingly punched Junior in the arm and told him to have a good day at school, and he left for work. Sam was always so upbeat and positive. He was just a joy to be around, and it was always so obvious why he and Dad were such good friends.

After Dad came outside, he handed Junior and me a couple of folded napkins. Inside the napkins were buttered biscuits with bacon and some of Mama's famous fig preserves. I always knew it was going to be a good day when it started with a breakfast like that. Dad told us to load up while he went inside to get Anna. I started the truck so it would have time to warm up before we left for school.

Dad and Anna finally came out as Junior and I were finishing our biscuits. We made room for them in the single-cab truck, and although we were packed in like sardines, everyone seemed to be comfortable. As we were going down the driveway, we saw Grandma flagging us down from her front porch. I wasn't sure if something was wrong or if she just needed something from town. Dad pulled up to her front yard and went up on the porch to talk with her.

Grandma and Dad talked for a minute before he made his way back to the truck. She seemed to be distressed, and I could tell something was wrong. When Dad got back in the truck, I asked him what was going on. He said, "Your grandma thinks she is really sick. She said she isn't feeling well."

I always wondered how she made it through the winters in that small cabin. Dad would often tell her to come stay with us, but she never did. Mama said she was stubborn and stuck in her ways. We would always take her bundles of firewood and leave them on her front porch. During the winter, we could often find her cuddled up in a blanket without a fire to keep her warm. The strong-willed woman that I had always known had somehow quickly changed into a feeble old woman. She never asked for help, even if she needed it.

Dad seemed worried as he drove us to school that morning, and he didn't say much. He was breathing fast as we approached Hargrove Lane on our left. Normally, we drove straight past the dirt road, but he slammed on the brakes and turned the truck around. As the red dust filled the truck, we all wanted to ask what he was doing, but after an awkward silence, he said, "One day away from school isn't going to kill anybody. If your Grandma is sick, we need to get her moved over to our house and call Dr. Moore."

Even with Grandma being sick, Dad was still aggravated that he would miss a day's work. It was not easy for him to turn that truck around and break away from our daily routines and responsibilities. He was devoted to his plans when it came to work, and it took something catastrophic to shift his attention. This was obviously a serious situation and all of his time and energy would be poured into taking care of his mother.

On the way back, Dad started slowing down as we drove up to the local gas and gossip station.

"Why are we stopping?" I asked.

"I've got to grab some chewing tobacco, but ya'll come on in and get what you want."

Our spirits were immediately lifted when Dad reminded us that they had Baby Ruth bars and RC Colas. The Little Brown Jug is what everyone called the small store, and we normally avoided it because it was a hangout for the McCrae's. Dad had quit chewing tobacco years before, and I was very surprised to see him stopping at the Jug, but I did not question him because of the circumstances. I reckon he thought a good chew of tobacco would calm his nerves. Unfortunately, we stopped at the wrong place at the wrong time.

When we walked inside, the small store was filled with cigar smoke. Dad walked up to the counter while telling us to hurry up and grab whatever we wanted. The three of us ran to the back of the store and pulled three cold RC Colas out of the cooler. Dad was talking to the owner, Mrs. Bennett, as we walked up. There were already three Baby Ruth chocolate bars and a pouch of Red Man chewing tobacco on the counter when we added our bottles.

Dad and Mrs. Bennett's conversation was then interrupted by a familiar voice that came from behind us. William's father, Billy McCrae, was sitting on a stool smoking a cigar. My heart started racing as soon as I thought about Dad and the kind of day he was having.

"You gonna buy that nigger boy's stuff too? Hell, he's like your son too, ain't he?"

"Is that supposed to be some kind of insult, Billy?" Dad asked.

"No, it was just an honest question. I just want to know why the Harrisons would rather hang around a bunch of no-good niggers than the rest of the fine people in this community."

"Well, if your character resembles that of those you speak of, then I don't have much use for them either." Billy quickly stood from his stool, and two other men emerged from the shadows behind him. He confidently approached Dad and did not stop until they were nose to nose. Dad waved the smoke out of his face and quickly shoved Billy in the chest.

"I don't want any problems here today, Billy. I'm running on a short fuse, and I'm not having the best day."

"If you put your hands on me again, it will be the last time," Billy said.

"Where was all of this confidence when you stopped by my place?" Dad asked.

"We both know you and that nigger Sam would have jumped on me."

"About like you have these two fine gentlemen with you here today, huh?" Dad asked.

The two large men were slowly making their way closer to Dad when we heard the hammer of a pistol being cocked. Mrs. Bennett proudly held a revolver over the counter and pointed it in the direction of Dad and Billy. The two men stopped advancing forward and clutched the pistols at their sides.

"I'm not going to have this kind of mess in my store! Billy, if you want to eat your breakfast in here anymore, then you leave these folks alone. Henry, take the children and go."

We quickly fell in line behind Dad and followed him out the front door as Billy hurled insults our way. Dad slammed the truck in gear and spun out in the rocks as we hurried toward home. After we made it out of there and he made sure we were all okay, Dad jokingly said, "Ya'll remind me not to go in there anymore."

Anna didn't seem to be too worried about it as she ate her chocolate bar, but I could tell that it bothered Junior. When we pulled up to Grandma's house, he couldn't hold it in any longer. "How come y'all's family is always at it with the McCraes?"

Dad answered, "You just got a good taste of what Billy McCrae and his family are like. I reckon he doesn't like us because we aren't scared to stand up to him. It is a long story, but there are some things that they still have not forgiven us for. The truth is that they think they are better than us, and they always have. Now, y'all come inside and let's check on your grandma."

Before we could get out, Junior said, "Hold up a minute. Mr. Henry, you ain't always got to take up for me like that. I think that man's problem is with me more than it is with you."

"He does not even know you, Junior. He does not know that you are polite and respectful. Billy's problem is his hateful, racist heart. He doesn't like anyone who doesn't look like him. Don't tell me I don't have to protect you if you are riding in my truck, son. Your daddy would do the same for John and Anna."

Mama was inside with Grandma, sitting by a warm fire in the living room. Grandma was staring into the fire and did not speak to any of us as we all came into the house. Usually, she greeted me with a warm smile and a hug. I didn't understand how she had become so sick just since the last time that I saw her.

Mama said, "John, come over here and speak to your Grandmother." Junior and I walked over to her, and I greeted her with a hug. I thought she was crying, but then I realized the tears were actually beads of sweat running down her face. She softly said, "There is my handsome grandson. I'm sorry that you have to see me like this."

After a few moments of sitting with her and watching her stare into the fire, Dad called Junior and me back to Grandma's room. He said, "You two are going to help me move this bed and her chest so we can make sure Mama is comfortable."

We made multiple trips back and forth and got everything she would need moved into our house. After we made sure Grandma was comfortable in her bed, an unfamiliar vehicle approached the house. Moments later, a tall, thin gentleman walked through the front door carrying a black bag.

Dad introduced him as Dr. Moore. The last time that I had seen him was when he helped Mama the day Anna was born. He put a stethoscope up to Grandma's chest and listened to her breathing. After he removed the stethoscope and checked her temperature, he stood up and called Mama and Dad outside.

A few minutes later, they came back inside and walked into the kitchen to gather themselves for a moment before coming back into the living room. Wiping tears from his eyes, Dad came back into the room and told us that Grandma was very sick and that we needed to pray. I asked Mama how bad it was, and she said, "John, Dr. Moore said Louise has an advanced case of pneumonia, and he doesn't know if she will live much longer." It felt like someone had knocked the wind out of me, and warm tears began to run down my face.

Junior put his arm around me, and when I looked over at him, he too had tears running down his face. "Man, I'm here for you, and you know that I love Miz Louise like she is my own grandmother," he said.

Mama said, "John, I understand that you are sad just like we all are, but I don't want Louise to see us crying. We need to make sure her last days here with us are happy days. She deserves that." So, I walked outside for a moment and sat on the swing to gather myself.

A few moments later, Dad walked outside and sat down on the swing beside me. "Are you alright, son?"

I just nodded my head because I couldn't come up with the right words. "This is hurting me just as bad as it is hurting you," he said. "We need to stay strong for your grandma and just make sure that she is comfortable."

All I could do was nod my head and say, "Yes, sir."

"You haven't been hunting in a while. Maybe you can take the rest of Christmas break to get us some deer meat and spend time with your grandma."

I knew he was trying his best to comfort me, but what normally would have made me happy didn't seem to have much of an effect. I had never dealt with losing someone close to me, and the thought of losing Grandma terrified me. As I sat outside on the swing, all I could think to do was to pray and ask God to give us all peace in our hearts.

Shortly after I prayed, Sam pulled in. Junior walked out and met Sam in the yard to tell him about Grandma. When Sam walked up on the porch, he came over and sat beside me on the swing. "How is she doing?" I told him what Dr. Moore had told my parents, and I could see that he was visibly shaken.

He said, "John, your grandma is probably the toughest woman that I know. Growing up, she could outwork most of the men around here. I hope you know that she will fight until the end." Sam's kind words were meant to help, but somehow they broke my heart. I was not ready to let go of her. I had so much that I wanted to tell her about finding the journal.

"Is your dad inside?" Sam asked.

"Yes, sir, I will walk you in." When we walked through the door, and Dad saw Sam, he broke down in tears. Sam walked over to the side of the bed and hugged Dad. I was confident that he was keeping Dad from falling to the floor.

After they embraced each other for what seemed like an eternity, Sam dropped to his knees and prayed for God's will to be done, and for peace and comfort. Grandma had touched so many lives, and obviously, Sam's was one of those.

When he had finished praying, Grandma reached her hand out and placed it in his. Sam's large hand seemed to swallow hers. She softly said, "I love you like a son, Sam. Thank you for being such a good friend to my boy."

For the rest of the evening, all our family stayed in the living room with Grandma. That was the only time I can remember that we didn't sit down and eat dinner together. We took turns feeding the fire and keeping a cool rag on Grandma's forehead.

Later that night, only Dad and I remained by her side. I had fallen asleep on the couch for a short period of time, and when I awoke, Dad was asleep in a chair by the bed. I went over and shook him to wake him up. I told him to go get in bed and that I would stay by Grandma's side for the rest of the night. He kissed her on the forehead, mumbled something under his breath, and made his way to the bedroom.

The next morning, Mama shook me to wake me up. "She made it through the night. Thanks for staying by her side," Mama said. Then she came over and stood behind me while running her fingers through my hair.

"It sure doesn't feel like Christmas Eve."

I replied, "Well, no matter what, at least we are all together. What if we eat our Christmas dinner and open our gifts tonight as a family while Grandma is still with us?"

"I like that idea," she said.

Dad had gone to break the news to my uncle and the rest of the family.

Not long after that, Dad came in, followed by my uncle, aunt and cousins, and my uncle asked us to give them some time to be alone with Grandma.

After that, we visited all day, and Dad told Uncle Lewis to run home and grab whatever gifts they had under the Christmas tree. It was a sad time, but if anyone was going to do his best to make it a happy time, it would be my father. It did not matter if we only had a few inexpensive gifts. What mattered is that we would all be gathered as a family in the presence of the woman who made it all possible.

Mama and Aunt Barbara went to work in the kitchen preparing a meal. My cousins and I went out back and started bringing firewood inside. The temperature was dropping quickly, and Christmas Day was going to be a cold one, but there was somehow a feeling of warmth in our house as Dad and Uncle Lewis rearranged the living room and placed gifts under the tree.

We set up the chairs in a circle around Grandma's bed and enjoyed our traditional family dinner. Grandma had become quiet and, for the most part, unresponsive. I kept my eyes on her left hand because it would tighten up and then release quite often, like she was trying to squeeze something.

Meanwhile, Dad and Uncle Lewis told stories about Christmas time growing up. They talked about how they would be lucky to receive apples and oranges for Christmas gifts, which made my cousins and me realize how blessed we were.

After we finished eating, Anna passed out gifts to everyone. Dad counted down from three, and we all started ripping the wrapping paper off and throwing it on the floor. Dad laughed, "Mama, I wish you could see how spoiled all of your grandchildren are!" I got a new pair of overalls and a brand new pair of boots that I desperately needed.

A couple of hours later, everyone started winding down and getting ready to call it a night. The past few hours had been full of blessings, warmth and time with our family. Reality started to set in with all of us when we thought about this possibly being our last night with Grandma. My uncle, aunt and cousins all said their goodbyes to Grandma, and we all wished each other a Merry Christmas as they walked out the door.

Mama and Anna hugged Grandma and told her they loved her before going to bed. Dad attempted to sit up all night, pouring his heart out to her while she was still able to squeeze his hand. After Dad was out of gas and had nothing left, I told him to go get in bed with Mama and Anna.

I threw some more wood on the fire and lay down beside Grandma, placing my index finger in her left hand. I told her how much I loved her and I promised her that I would take care of Tripod and the cats despite what Dad might say about it. I also thanked her for all of the things that she had done for me.

At some point, I fell asleep beside Grandma. When the song birds woke me, I realized that she had stopped squeezing my finger. She was cold and no longer breathing.

7

SAYING GOODBYE

Grandma Louise left us behind and went home to be with the Lord and Grandpa Pat. The thought of her being in heaven with Grandpa Pat brought me peace. She knew how we felt and how loved she was, but now she was feeling the most pure love that a person could ever feel in the presence of God.

Around lunchtime on Christmas Day, when it had warmed up some, we met with family and close friends to go bury Grandma. Five or six vehicles followed us to the north end. We would lay her to rest under a giant oak tree right beside Grandpa Pat.

When we pulled into the pasture and drove around to the old oak tree, I saw Sam and Junior sitting in the shade of the tree. They had already dug a hole beside Grandpa. Clearly, the Harrisons were not the only people to lose a family member that morning.

Everyone made their way across the pasture and parked under the massive oak tree, and a few minutes later, cars started pouring in through the gate. I realized that every family getting out of the cars was from the colored community. I recognized a lot of them from seeing Dad speak to them in the past, but some of the older ones, I did not know. Dad and

Uncle Lewis were obviously getting emotional as Sam brought up the different families to pay their respects to Grandma. Every local who knew her took time out of their Christmas Day to join us.

Every family that came to pay their respects said nearly the same thing. They all said that they loved Grandma and appreciated everything that she had done for them. They told stories, laughed, and joked until it was time, then they asked for the honor of lowering Grandma into the ground, so Dad and Uncle Lewis could sit. At a time of such racial division, it was a blessing to see white and black families come together at a funeral.

When we lowered Grandma into the dark soil under the oak tree, a slight breeze began to blow out of the North. With the wind picking up at the exact time she was lowered into the ground, it seemed like the Lord was there with us. Coincidence or not, everyone looked up and acknowledged that it was an amazing moment. I knew Grandma was happy, and I did not know if my tears were of sadness or happiness.

After the funeral, Dad invited some people over to the house to eat. Sam, Junior, and their entire family came to our house, but my mind was on something else. I explained to Junior that I wanted to carry the journal that we had found to the woods with me so I could read it. I asked him to keep his eyes open for me while I snuck to the barn and retrieved the journal. I left it outside, hidden under the hay, while I went inside and asked Dad to give me the deer rifle so I could go hunting.

Dad asked, " Are you sure that you don't want to stay here with Junior this evening?"

Before I could reply, Sam spoke up and said, "Let the boy go hunting. He deserves some alone time." Dad agreed with Sam, so we walked back to his room, and he pulled the rifle from under the mattress on his bed.

It was a beautiful lever-action Marlin 336 chambered in .30-30. For the most part, Dad had grown up hunting with shotguns, but he had bought this rifle in 1948. Over the last eleven years, it had become his favorite deer gun, and I had fallen in love with it as well. Dad handed me four cartridges and told me if I needed more than that, I needed to target practice more often. I had already killed my fair share of deer, but he never hesitated to remind me that he was a better shot than I was.

Afterward, I walked into my room and leaned the rifle up against the wall. There were a few things that I considered necessities when I went to the woods, and I needed to take them all. I couldn't forget Pat's skinning knife, along with a flashlight and an old set of rattling antlers. After I had placed them all in my pack and changed clothes, I grabbed the rifle and headed toward the living room.

As badly as I wanted to sneak out the back door, I knew speaking to everyone first was the honorable thing to do. I figured out at an early age that Dad was always watching me to make sure that I was polite and respectful. I knew it was better to slow down and do things right the first time because if I didn't, he would be there to correct me. He always told me it's better to do something right the first time.

The moment I had been waiting for was fast approaching. The open screen door seemed like a gateway to freedom and a getaway from everything that had been going on. Before I could make it out the back door, Dad grabbed my pack and stopped me in my tracks. He asked, "Where are you going to sit this afternoon?"

"I'm going to sit in the bottom below the barn where Junior and I saw all of the fresh deer sign." He told me to be careful and to come home and get him if I shot a deer.

When my feet hit the grass, I made a straight line to the barn and grabbed the journal. Placing it in my pack, I walked down the tree line toward Mason Road. The slight breeze and chill in the air calmed my nerves as I took a deep breath. The temperature was dropping fast, and that meant that the deer movement would be good. Finally, I was on my way to a place where I could sit in silence and read Pat's journal.

I made my way down the edge of Mason Road and crossed over Wasden Road. Even though I was tempted to stop at the first shade tree I saw and read the journal, I pressed on. After crossing the first two hay fields, I came to the bottom and followed the stream around to where Junior and I had previously left the shovel. I began to see more deer sign as I followed the ridge around toward the big bottom. The only thing left for me to do was to find a good spot to sit down.

The view was beautiful in that section of woods. There was a mix of oak, hickory, ash, and black walnut trees. It was fairly thick in the bottom, but the ridge was wide open and the trees were spread out. Looking around, I knew it was the perfect spot to spend the rest of the afternoon.

Making my way to the top of the ridge, I checked the wind direction. It was blowing directly in my face. I knew that the deer would most likely be in the bottom, so I sat down by a blown-over tree. My back was to the field with the blown-over tree behind me, so the deer would not be able to pick me off. Staying quiet and concealed was very important, and both played a huge role in being successful. These were things that my father had taught me from an early age.

Once I sat down, I pulled a small limb over my legs to further camouflage myself. I was tucked in and very confident that the deer would not be able to see me. I placed my pack just to my right and laid the Marlin rifle over my lap. It was finally time to relieve my curiosity, so I reached into my pack and pulled out the journal.

It was an indescribable feeling to put my hands on the journal free of worry. I was excited to have the next few hours to settle in and read with no distractions. Even though I claimed to be there to kill a deer, I was truly there to read about my family's treasure.

I had waited for what felt like an eternity to see what was important enough to be buried in the woods. If it was considered to be a treasure by my grandfather, then it had to be something that would change my life forever. I opened the journal to the first page and became lost in my grandfather's words.

8

PAT HARRISON- APRIL, 1865

It was just after my thirteenth birthday, and to this day I can still smell the smoke. I remember the panic in my mother's voice as the first of many torches shattered our window and landed at her feet. When we could no longer breathe, we went outside to plead with the Union officers. We offered them everything in our possession if they would stop torching the house. Unfortunately, there was not a soul there who could convince them to spare our home.

My father, "Doc" Harrison, flew the American flag when we heard the Yankees were on their way to Selma and burning everything in their path. He and my grandfather were accused of being "Union men" by the locals because they did not support secession. My grandfather Lewis convinced Pa not to take us, along with our valuables, and leave the farm. He claimed that the Yankees would not burn the farm if they saw the Union flag. He was sorely mistaken, and my family suffered greatly at the hands of Wilson's raiders in April of eighteen sixty-five.

Even though my father was against slavery and had not chosen sides, I quickly began to hate those men in the dark blue uniforms. They laughed and cursed as they burned everything that we had worked for. They saw nothing wrong with taking our bacon, flour, and corn. They were savages as far as I was concerned, and they had no hearts beating inside their chests. My optimistic father told me to be thankful that they were sparing our lives, but I could see nothing other than violence and hatred.

Mason, my younger brother, was sick and on his deathbed, and they still showed no mercy. When my mother pleaded with the captain on horseback, he told her that he was "just following orders." Before they came down the road in between the giant oak trees, their minds were made up. The only things that they did not take from us were our own lives. They stole everything from cows, horses, and crops to the blankets my mother had made for us.

As each Billy Yank walked by me, I was tempted to pull the Bowie knife that was hidden in my waistline. I knew that was not an option because a move like that would be committing suicide. There were at least fifty of them and only a few of us. Nathan Bedford Forest's Confederate forces were forty miles northwest of us in Selma, but to the Confederates, we were an enemy because my father made it known that we could not and would not support the Confederacy.

If it were not for our connections through my mother's side of the family, we surely would not have made it through the war. Her uncle was Judge Rueben Saffold in downtown Montgomery, and her father was a very wealthy planter with connections in high places. Because my father was very vocal about opposing slavery, they were the ones who kept the mob from kicking down our front door. Thank the good Lord that it never came to that. We were living in a beautiful home on my grandfather James Smith's plantation. He was very well known and very wealthy. For that reason, people did not view us as much of a threat. James had given my mother Molly a portion of his Bellewood Plantation as a wedding gift and had a home built there for her and my father. Grandfather James relied upon the hard labor of nearly one hundred slaves on two large tracts of land. As Pa used to say, " He had more money than he knew what to do with." He insisted that my father accept twenty-five of his own slaves to help him break the dirt and start a farming operation, but my father refused and took all of the work upon his own shoulders.

I remember feeling helpless and hopeless as I watched our home crumble into ashes. I felt angry and provoked as I watched them load up the wagons with every bit of food that we had. I knew that we would be starting over. Sitting at the base of a pear tree in the yard, I knew life was about to get hard for our family. The Yankees left as fast as they came, and they left us in a heap of ashes and sorrow. In the distance, I could see smoke rising, and I knew that the Yankees had likely burned my grandfather James's plantation home.

My grandfather Lewis, on my father's side, was a silversmith and president of the Montgomery Eufaula railroad. He had built a home in downtown Montgomery in 1830 when he came here from Maine. We relied heavily upon his deep pockets to help us rebuild our lives in the years following Wilson's raid. I believe he felt that he owed it to my father since he told him not to flee before the Yankees arrived.

Lewis was a self-made man who worked for everything that he had, and he taught my father to be the same way. He was also a God fearing man, and he did not spare the rod when it came to the people that he loved. Being a preacher and a former surgeon, my father often stuck out like a sore thumb. He received his medical education at the University of New York, but hadn't practiced in a long time. He did not drink, cuss, smoke, or gamble, and because of that, men looked at him differently.

Grandpa Lewis helped my father come up with the funds to build a small church about half of a mile from where we lived. Some Sundays, it was just our immediate family that gathered there. On other Sundays, we would have small crowds who were often uncomfortable when Pa preached against slavery. I learned from a young age that the truth often hurts people's feelings. I knew it was the truth because Pa read it straight from the Word of God.

I never understood how people could claim to be Christians, but also support slavery. I knew that we were called to love one another and serve one another. I did not understand why people viewed other people as property and only wanted to be constantly served. My father used to say it was all about money and self-gain. He often preached against that at church as well. I imagine it could have become a large church if Pa had just told everyone what they wanted to hear.

My grandfather James would show up every now and then, and he would often leave with a look of disgust on his face. He was a very wealthy man, but to admit that he was wrong would cause him to lose everything that he had. The last time we saw him at church, he had gotten up and left in the middle of my father's sermon. I knew Mama worried about where he would spend eternity and if his heart would ever be softened. Sadly, I knew his heart was not in the right place when he left this world.

As I leaned up against the tree, I began to feel as if I was going to pass out from exhaustion. Just as everything around me began to fade away, I heard gunshots ring out in the distance. The shots had come from the direction of the main plantation house. I wondered if I was dreaming, but when Pa ran past me in that direction, I fell in behind him, struggling to keep up.

We jumped the board fence and crossed the pasture as quickly as we could. My grandparent's home was a half mile from our place and on the other side of a large swamp. Once we crossed the pasture, we came to the edge of the swamp, and Pa never slowed down. Out of breath, I followed in his footsteps.

The huge cypress trees in the swamp painted a beautiful picture. Even in the daylight, seeing the beautiful swamp did not help with the uneasy feeling that was coming over me. I knew what creatures lurked below the surface of that old swamp. I was thinking about a loggerhead turtle biting my foot in half when I heard Pa say, "Come on, boy! What are you waiting for?" Truth be told, I was probably waiting for him to change his mind and turn around.

As we were wading through the murky water of the swamp, Pa told me to keep my eyes open for snakes. For the first time in my life, I wasn't worried about them. I knew that I could see a cottonmouth floating on the surface. It was what I could not see under the water that gave me an eerie feeling.

Out of breath, I tried to ignore the thought of what we would discover on the other side. Both of my boots had filled with water, and it became a challenge to pull them out of the mud. Just when I was ready to stop and take a break, I noticed Pa had reached the other side. With his hands on his knees, he urged me to hurry across.

When I reached the other side, the familiar smell of smoke filled my nostrils. All of a sudden, embers were floating in the air as if it were snowing. Pa quickly turned around, grabbed me, and pulled me to the ground. We lay flat on the ground, and the only thing that I could hear was my heart beating rapidly. I whispered, "Pa, what are we doing?"

He replied, "The Yanks are leaving. Keep your head down."

A few moments passed, and I slowly raised my head as Pa crawled closer to the tree line. I could see a long line of soldiers making their way down the road and away from us. Behind them were James's horses, mules, and too many slaves to count. Some owere on wagons, and some were walking behind the convoy. I could hear the awful sounds of children crying and the soldiers talking back and forth.

Pa and I hid in the edge of the tree line for a while, but we eventually made our way out of the woods. We cautiously snuck around the horse barn, and Pa slowly peeked around the corner. I heard him say to himself, "God have mercy, everything is gone." When we eased out into the open, I could not believe my eyes. My grandparents' home had been reduced to a pile of hot coals and ashes.

As we approached, the warmth from the red-hot coals was almost too much to bear. It was extremely quiet around what used to be a buzzing, magnificent home. The enslaved families' living quarters and the horse barn were all that remained. The main barn that sat out behind the house had been burned to the ground.

Pa and I carefully made our way around the perimeter of the fire, struggling to see through the embers and smoke. When we got close to the brick foundation of the chimney, Pa suddenly stopped and put his hand on my chest as if he had heard something. Through the popping and crackling of the fire, we heard what sounded like a loud clicking noise. We looked at each other and slowly moved in that direction.

I could barely see Pa through the smoke when he yelled, "My God, it is James." He quickly disappeared into the smoke and started calling me for help. When I got to him, I saw my Grandfather lying in his own blood. He was holding a revolver to his head and repeatedly pulling the trigger. Pa took the pistol from him, and I dragged him out in the yard and away from the smoke. Once we got to where we could see, we realized how bad it was.

We saw the wounds under his blood-soaked shirt, and they looked to be fatal. Grandpa was trying his best to talk, but he was fading fast and had lost a lot of blood. He was as pale as a ghost, and there was no life in his eyes. He began to whisper, and we leaned down to see if we could hear what he was saying. Just before he passed, he whispered, "Find Elizabeth."

Carefully laying Grandpa's head in the grass, Pa looked at me and said, "Your grandmother is here somewhere. We have to find her."

"She must have been able to sneak away before the Yankees arrived," I thought. We combed the woods around the house, but there was no sign of her. There was too much ground to cover by foot, so we agreed to go to the old barn in the back, hoping the Yankees had overlooked it.

About halfway back to the barn, we saw fresh wagon tracks in the mud. Seeing the tracks seemed to make Pa walk faster. "Come on, boy. We've got to find your grandmother in before dark, and we need horses." After we walked nearly a mile, we reached the old barn by the cotton fields. "The horses are all still here," Pa said. Sure enough, when we turned the corner, every horse was in its stall and had not been disturbed.

Pa and I found two saddles and began to look for two good horses. We both nearly jumped out of our skin when we heard someone scream, "Doc, up here!" Above us in the attic of the old barn, we heard footsteps running towards the ladder. Pa ran over and helped my Grandmother Elizabeth down the ladder along with three of her servants.

"I've lost everything. This is too much to bear," Grandmother Elizabeth said as she fell into Pa's arms. She then told us about how James refused to leave the plantation house. From the cover of the woods, she sat and watched as the Yankees dragged her husband from their home and left him for dead. After that, she said Lucy snuck her to the wagon and took her to the barn where her children were hiding.

Pa asked where the rest of the negroes were, and Lucy told us that some of them ran away, but most of them went with the soldiers. Lucy, her daughter Nan, and her son Joe were the only three remaining servants on the plantation. According to Lucy, even the overseers hit the woods when they got word that the Yankees were coming. On a piece of property where there were normally over one hundred people, only six remained.

Pa and I went just behind the barn and brought the wagon around from where it was hidden. He then told me to finish saddling the two horses. After I was finished, Pa said, "Well, if there is one good thing about today, it is the fact that you and Joe both have your own horses now."

Before I could wrap my head around what Pa had just said, they were gone down the trail in the wagon. I looked at Joe and said, "Guess we'd better mount up." We jumped on our new horses, and together, we fell in behind them.

As we slowly made our way down the trail back toward the front of the property, I looked over at Joe. "I've seen you around, but I don't think that we have met," I said.

Joe replied, "Well, I'm Joe and I know who you are. I've seen you around the big house a few times with Pastor Doc." I told him how the plantation house had been burned down, then we rode in silence from there on. Both of our lives had just changed so much, and I imagine Joe had as much on his mind as I did.

The closer we got to the smoke, the more curious I became about what Pa was going to do. How was he going to play this hand that we had been dealt? I was just thankful that I was not the leader of our family at that moment. If it had been up to me, we would have already died in a shootout with the Yankees when the first torch was thrown on our home. Unfortunately, at that age, I did not possess the patience, mercy, or grace that my father possessed.

I could hear Grandmother wailing as we approached what used to be her home. When the wagon came to a stop, she ran over to the dead body of my grandfather. She slowly sat down on the green grass there in the backyard and said her goodbyes to him. I don't know if she was sad or angry, but she sure gave Grandpa a good cussing. We gave her all of the time that she needed and then loaded the body on the wagon so that Mama could say her goodbyes as well. What Pa and I had seen and heard was enough for any man, but we were still faced with the task of telling my mother that she would never talk to her father again.

Pa pulled me to the side and asked me if I had seen the wounds in James's back. I walked back over to the wagon and took a peek while Grandma was not looking. There appeared to be multiple stab wounds about halfway up his back. Pa whispered, "Looks like the Yankees put the bayonets to him and left him to bleed out." Thankfully, Grandmother didn't see the severity of the wounds, and we were praying that Mama wouldn't see it when we got James's body back home.

Pa told Lucy that if she didn't have anywhere to go, she may as well bring her family to stay with us since we had all lost everything. I don't think Grandmother Elizabeth could have made it a day without Lucy at her side anyway. I had seen Joe, Lucy, and Nan at the main house, but James wouldn't allow us to become acquainted. Lucy accepted Pa's offer and made it clear that Joe and Nan would help out however they could. Afterward, we headed toward what used to be our home.

As we made our way down the road, Joe said, "Mama said they burned y'all's house down, too."

I replied, "Yeah, it was probably the same Yanks that burned down the big house."

"Where y'all gonna live now?" Joe asked.

"I'm not sure, but I bet Pa has a plan," I replied. That same morning, I was fishing on the creek without a worry in the world, and that afternoon, I didn't know where I would lay my head. As much as I wanted to feel sorry for myself, I also saw how much it was hurting Joe and his family.

When we made it around the turn, I could still see smoke coming from our place up on the hill. As we got closer, Pa sped up the wagon and then yelled loudly, "Molly!"

That's when I noticed Mama sitting under the shade tree with Mason lying across her lap. I jumped from the horse as quickly as I could. Mama was still crying, and my brother's body seemed to be lifeless in her lap. She said, "He didn't make it. The smoke got to him."

Pa and I both fell to the ground at Mama's feet, and I cried like I never had before. First, they took my Grandfather, and now my little brother, all on the same day. Mason was five years old, puny, and weak. The doctors never could tell us what was wrong with him. With him being as sick as he was, none of us knew how long he would live, but I didn't expect him to leave us so early. The more I tried to look at my brother, the harder it became to accept what had just happened. I had never felt that kind of pain in my life.

Pa picked Mason up, carried him over to the wagon, and laid him down beside James. Elizabeth was trying to comfort Mama when Pa called Mama over to the wagon. Before he could say a word, Mama saw Grandpa James, fell to the ground, and screamed at God. Pa then told me and Joe to run down to the creek and get some water for the horses. As we were walking away, I could hear Mama questioning God, screaming, "Why?"

Joe didn't say much to me as we walked down to the creek, but I could tell that he had a lot to say. We had just met an hour before, but it seemed like we had already been through so much together. For some reason, I felt like I had known him my entire life. Maybe I felt like that because I knew he had been through some horrible things in his life, too. Deep down, I was glad that he was there.

Reaching the creek, Joe and I dipped our buckets into the cool water. The water that was running downstream slowly filled our buckets, and I began to feel a bit of relief. "Have you ever been fishing in this creek, Joe?" I asked.

Joe smirked and said, "No, Master James didn't like for us to wander off too far."

"Well, maybe we can rig up some cane poles and come back down here before long," I replied. I think holding on to the idea of fishing brought me temporary peace because I knew I was about to bury my brother and Grandfather.

When Joe and I came back up the hill, everybody was still under the shade tree and next to the wagon. After we watered the horses, Pa told us to go get a couple of shovels and hurry back. Then he told us that we would be going back to James's family cemetery to bury the bodies and that we would have to hurry to get it done before dark. I reckon Mama and Pa decided to go ahead and bury them because of the destruction that the Yankees had caused. There was not enough time or any possible way to get everyone together.

Joe and I followed the wagon on horseback as we made our way to the cemetery. I had only been there a couple of times when I was younger. After we passed the big house and rode up to the cemetery, I thought to myself, "This is an awfully pretty place to go at such a sad time." The huge pecan trees had been watching over that cemetery for a very long time.

Mama and Grandma Elizabeth picked a spot, and we started digging. After we got past the roots, the dirt seemed to be as soft as butter. After about an hour of digging, Pa, Joe and I had the holes dug. We slowly lowered the bodies into the ground and let the women say their goodbyes. As much as I was hurting, I was trying to be strong like Pa.

After Mama and Grandma Elizabeth had their time, Pa and I stepped up and said goodbye to Mason. I tried my best not to cry, but all of the memories I had with my little brother were too much to bear. My heart seemed like it was a lump in my throat, and I felt like I was going to pass out. Pa came over, hugged me, and said, "Son, it's time." He put a shovel in my hand, and with the dark approaching, we filled the holes.

That night, we slept in one of the servants' cabins behind the big house. We simply did not have anywhere else to go. Mama and Grandma Elizabeth slept in the two small beds, and Pa and I slept on the floor. We could have slept in a different cabin in a bed, but Pa said we needed to stay close to Mama and Grandma. Lucy, Nan and Joe slept in the cabin next to us.

As I lay on the hard floor in the dark, I thought about how we had never slept in a place like that, but Joe and his family did it every night. Within a day, everything had changed. We had lost it all. Life as we knew it would never be the same. It was time to rebuild.

9

The Enemy

The next morning, the sound of creaking boards woke me from a dead sleep. I saw Pa slowly sneaking towards the front door of the small cabin. He quietly began to slip his boots on, and he eased out the door. My back felt like I had been run over by a herd of angry cattle, and I swore to never sleep on a wooden floor again.

No matter how bad things had gotten, I knew Pa would lead us in the right direction. I was eager to go outside and see what he had planned for the day. I quietly made my way to the door and put my boots on. As I opened the door, I realized the sun had not yet risen. The burning embers from the house were still glowing in the low light, and the song birds were singing like our whole life had not just crumbled before our eyes. I guess their lives had not changed for the worse, and if you asked them, it was the beginning of a good day.

Pa was sitting in the old wooden rocking chair at the end of the porch. I believe I interrupted his morning prayer, but he didn't seem to mind too much. He said, "Heck of a sight, isn't it?"

"Yes, sir, I never thought it would come to this."

"Well, it is the hand that we have been dealt, son, and we will have faith that God is going to provide," he said. I often admired Pa's faith in the midst of our battles.

While Pa and I were talking, Joe came out of the cabin next to us and quietly eased the door closed. I imagined that on a normal day, Joe would have begun working around that time. Most likely, he would have gone to the fields or done whatever he was told to do. Surely, that is why he looked so confused as he stood and stared at the glowing embers. He was lost, just like the rest of us.

Pa called out, "Good morning, Joe. Come over here." Joe cautiously walked in our direction without making eye contact. Pa continued, "Joe, I'm going to Montgomery today to talk with my father, and I need you to help Pat around here. I've given him some chores to do today while I am away." Joe quietly replied, "Yes, sir, whatever you need."

"No, Joe, it isn't just about us. You've got a mother and a sister to take care of now. Whatever work you do with my family will be for all of us."

Joe, with a surprised look on his face, quickly nodded his head. I couldn't help but smile because while it seemed that our freedom was being stripped from us, Joe seemed to be finding his.

Pa said, "Tell your mama that I'm riding to town to talk to your Grandpa Lewis. I'll be back as soon as I can. Oh, yeah, and Pat, watch over things until I get back." He gave me a look that I knew very well as he mounted his horse. I knew that he meant business, and I felt the weight of that responsibility as Pa rode off into the low morning light.

I was hoping that Pa had plans to bring food and supplies back from town. All we had left to our name were the things that he had hidden before the Yankees arrived. He had given me some chores to do that morning, but as I looked at mine and Joe's dirty clothes, I had an idea. "Hey, Joe, is your mama still asleep?"

"Far as I know, she is," Joe replied. I knew we had a little while until everyone woke up, so I figured it was time for a little bit of fun. The cloud of doom and gloom that had been hovering over us was enough to deprive any man of his joy.

"Come on, Joe," I said, as I took off running towards the creek. After a few moments, I realized that Joe wasn't coming with me. I turned around and asked, "Well, are you coming or not?"

Joe was looking at me like I was stupid. Then, he said, "I ain't too big on running towards them woods, Pat." It hit me that Joe didn't feel comfortable about what I was trying to do, and I felt foolish for a moment.

I walked back over to Joe and asked, "Have you ever been fishin' ?"

"Nah, I've helped Mama clean a few for Master Smith."

"Well, what do you say we go try to catch a few for breakfast?"

"Your Pa ain't gonna be mad if we go down there?" Joe asked.

"Pa ain't here, and Mama and them are still asleep. Come on, let's go. We ain't gonna get in trouble,"

I assured Joe. Reluctantly, Joe agreed and we made our way down past the cabins and toward what the Creek Indians had named the Pintlala Creek.

The Upper Creek Indians had used the bountiful swamps of Pintlala to hunt, fish and trap. Pintlala comes from the word *pithlo*, meaning canoe, and the verb *halatas*, meaning to drag. I often found that humorous because I, too, had given up using a canoe in the summer months. The water was simply too shallow unless a good rain had passed through.

The sun still had not risen, and I knew we would be getting to the creek at the perfect time. The fish were always hungry at daybreak and sunset. After we covered a few hundred yards, we turned down the trail and toward the creek. As we left the field and entered the woods, our surroundings became much darker. Thankfully, we had a logging trail to follow in.

The sound of the woods waking up was always something that I looked forward to. I reckon it was because it made me feel close to God. I knew there had to be a God up there to create something as beautiful as the spring woods at daylight. My peaceful thoughts were interrupted by what sounded like a huge bull walking behind me. From that point on, I showed Joe how Pa had taught me to walk quietly in the woods.

I knew when the leaves started turning into white sand that we were getting close. Even at a young age, it seemed like the woods drained me of any negative thoughts. The timber and the dense green forest were like home to me. I felt like it was where I belonged and that I was born to be outdoors. That familiar feeling washed over me as we approached the creek bank.

I asked Joe to find two straight saplings that we could turn into fishing poles. While he worked at breaking the fresh, green saplings in two, I pulled the fishing line and hooks from my back pocket. No matter where I was, I always carried a knife, flint, fishing line, and hooks. Over the years, the habit that my Grandpa Lewis had taught me bailed me out of some difficult situations.

Joe brought the saplings over, and I began to remove the soft bark in long strips with my pocket knife. After a little elbow grease, the saplings had transformed into fishing poles. They were white in color and slick to the touch. A few inches down the poles, I whittled a groove so that the poles rested comfortably in our hands. After I admired my work for a moment and bragged to Joe, I tied the hooks and line to the end of the poles.

I slipped my muddy boots off and dug my toes into the cool, white sand. "Let's go. We still have to find bait."

As I eased into the clear, cold water, it began to wash the mud off my feet. My feet were blistered and raw from wearing the same boots through the swamp the day before. After the initial shock we both experienced from the cold water, Joe and I set out to find bait.

We moved slowly down the creek listening to the sounds of spring. The song birds were in full force, and the owls were going back and forth with each other. Just then, a familiar noise came from above the creek bed in the timber. It was a sound that stood out from the rest. I immediately stopped walking and began to try and locate where the sound was coming from.

Smiling, I looked at Joe and said, "That is a hen turkey. We are underneath their roost." Then Joe and I almost jumped out of our skin when a thunderous noise came from above us, even closer than the hen turkey. I had only heard that sound when I went turkey hunting with Pa. It was the unmistakable gobble of a wild tom. There weren't many around in those days, so it was a rare treat and one that we would cut our teeth on. My hair stood up on my arms and neck as I told Joe to back out slowly.

We slowly backtracked as the tom continued to gobble and shake the woods around us. Once we were around the bend and past where we started, I could not contain myself any longer. "Joe! We found a gobbler!" I said.

"I hear them all of the time back here in the mornings, Joe said.

"That was a turkey roost, and they are right on the creek. We can come back and hunt that tom when Pa gets back from town." Joe looked at me, not really understanding my excitement. Soon, he would fully see the power of a duel between two of God's finest creations.

We walked a little further and found an old, dead tree lying on the creek bank. Getting down on our hands and knees, we began to dig under the rotten log. "Got one!" Joe said. He pulled a big, white, juicy slug out from under the log and set it aside. The more we scoured the steep edge of the creek, the more slugs and worms we found. Before long, we had enough bait to try our luck.

Grinning at Joe, I said, "Well, the fish aren't going to catch themselves. We need to find a deep hole and start there."

Joe confidently smiled, "I'm ready when you are!" We then slowly eased down the creek and away from the gobbler that had my adrenaline pumping. After we had covered a couple of hundred yards, we walked up to a spot where a tree had fallen.

Where the root system had been was a deep hole, a perfect spot to drop our hooks. Out of the corner of my eye, I caught movement in the shallow water up ahead. "Don't move, Joe. There is a huge alligator gar up against the bank." I could see his fin sticking out of the water, and I knew that we had to catch him.

Pa and I had caught gar on set lines before, and I knew the big ones weren't anything to play around with. I told Joe to put the big slug he had found on his hook. "We need to throw your line past the fish and up towards the bank. When it hits the water, we are going to walk backwards until you drag it right past him."

Joe held the pole, and I snuck around with the hook in my hand. The big gar hadn't moved an inch as I imagined he was hunting for breakfast himself. I took the line and all of the slack and tossed it down the creek just past the fish. Slowly, I walked back behind Joe, and we began walking backward. The slack was eventually taken up, and the bait was headed right for the huge fish.

"He's sure to break your line if he bites that hook, so as soon as he takes the bait, run backwards as fast as you can," I said.

Joe looked focused and determined as he gripped the pole tighter. The slug rudely bumped the gar as it boldly came by, and the fish immediately turned and attacked the slug. Water splashed us in the faces as Joe snatched the pole and took off up the creek.

I could not tell that the fish was hooked until Joe started pulling. Sure enough, during the chaos, the big gar snapped the line like it wasn't even there. Unfortunately for him, he had made a fatal mistake. While he was fighting Joe, he flopped out of the deep hole and onto the sandbar with us. He had become vulnerable, and it was now or never.

Knowing the hook was no longer in his mouth, I sprang into action. The gar was only inches away from slipping back into the water before I ran over and grabbed him. The strength of the fish was unbelievable, and he nearly pulled me into the water with him. Reaching to my side, I grabbed my Bowie knife and stabbed the fish right behind the head, where Pa had taught me to. It was a quick and honorable death for the prehistoric-looking fish.

My adrenaline was pumping as I straddled the gar. I could not believe how large and thick the fish's scales were. "Lay down beside him!" Joe proudly said. We were both surprised when we saw that the behemoth was longer than I was. "How are we gonna get him back home?"

"I haven't thought that far ahead," I replied. I pulled my knife out of the fish and began to think of a way to efficiently transport the fish back home.

"Why don't you run home and bring the wagon back along with the water buckets? I will stay here and try to clean this fish while you are gone," I said. Joe agreed and made his way back toward the logging trail, eventually walking out of sight. I knew it was going to be nearly impossible to clean the fish with the knife that I had, but there was no other option. As badly as I wanted to sneak back down the creek and fool with that turkey, I decided it was best to be responsible and work on breakfast.

After attempting to puncture the thick scales of the gar along his spine multiple times, I was quickly becoming discouraged. Eventually, I figured out that I could bump the handle of the knife with my hand. With the extra force, I was able to puncture the thick scales and begin working straight down the spine. The thick, flaky, white meat was full of bones, but I knew Mama and Lucy could make quick work of it. After about thirty minutes, I had only made my way down one side of the fish.

I had seen Pa take a cleaver and go down the side of a gar in seconds and then remove what he referred to as the "backstrap" with a sharp knife. But it looked as if it was going to be quite a task for me with my knife, so I decided to wait for reinforcements. I leaned up against the creek bank and fell asleep until I eventually heard what I thought was dogs barking in the distance. They sounded like hunting dogs, and as the barking grew louder, I took cover in the thick brush.

Moments later, I could hear splashing in the creek around the bend. When I looked up, a healthy blue tick hound was trotting towards me with his nose in the air. He went straight to the gar that was lying on the sandbar and began sniffing the fish. I recognized the notch on the dog's ear as belonging to the McCraes.

As I sat there in silence, the hound lost interest and began making his way down the creek. I was more than sure that the fish, along with a wind that did not favor the hound, had covered my scent. As I lost sight of the hound, I could hear more dogs closing the distance between us. I decided to crawl backwards until I reached a large hickory tree. Slowly, I eased up to see if I could locate the dogs.

They sounded to be a couple of hundred yards away and moving in my direction, so I decided to sneak down the opposite side of the creek back to the logging trail. After a moment, I became impatient and began to run until I heard a man talking loudly up ahead of me. The dogs continued to close in from my right, and I heard the blue tick raising hell up ahead. When I came around the bend, I saw Joe, Mama, Elizabeth, Lucy, and Nan being held at gunpoint by two men on horseback.

My hand found the revolver at my hip. I sprang from the tree line and levelled the gun at the bigger man's chest. The horses reared in panic, hurling the younger rider into the dark water. "Whoa, boy, we are just having a talk," the older man said.

"Well, is there a reason you have that rifle pointed at my family, mister?" Just then, the other hounds crossed the creek and surrounded us. The man laughed, lowered his rifle, and placed it across his lap.

"You see, boy, we are looking for Mr. McCrae's property, and we have word that his niggers are hiding in this swamp," the man said.

"As far as I know, the creek is the property line, and we haven't heard anything about that. So you need to be on your way before my Pa shows up." When I mentioned Pa, the two men looked at each other and began laughing.

"You mean to tell me I am supposed to be worried about Doc Harrison, a preacher? Doc wouldn't harm a fly," the large man said.

"You don't know my Pa, and he won't appreciate you trespassing and holding his family at gunpoint."

"His family? It looks to be you, three niggers, and two old women to me." Before anyone could react, I cocked the hammer on my pistol and settled the bead on the man's head.

"Alright, alright, boy. We were just coming to have a conversation. We will be back. Come on, Will, let's go," the man said.

The young, clean-cut, red-headed man had a nasty look on his face as we locked eyes. He then knocked the sand from his clothes and mounted his horse, and they rode back across the creek. Just as they got out of sight, the man whistled, and the blue tick broke off Joe, and the rest of the hounds followed them through the swamp. The dogs had been trained to find runaway slaves, and if the man had given the command, I believe the blue tick would have tried to rip Joe to pieces. Everyone seemed to be frozen and hadn't said a word since I popped out of the bushes. They all looked as if they had seen a ghost.

"Do you know who those men were?" I asked. Lucy and Nan both looked like they wanted to say something, but they were too rattled to get the words out. "I'm gonna tell Pa when he gets home, and we are going to find out what they were talking about." I could feel the adrenaline pumping through my veins, but after the last few days, it seemed that I was able to control it better.

In an attempt to break the awkward silence, I said, "Well, come on and let's go get our fish." Joe and I led the mules down the shallow creek to where the huge alligator gar was lying. Lucy, Nan, Mama and Grandma Elizabeth all gasped as they saw the size of the prehistoric fish.

"How did y'all manage to catch that thing, Pat?" Mama asked.

"I reckon we just got lucky, but it ought to feed us until Pa gets home." Everybody but Mama and Grandma Elizabeth got off the wagon and helped me load the fish. With a smile on my face, I gave Joe a pat on the back and assured him that Pa would be proud of us.

After we made it back to the remains of the big house, I found a shovel and began shoveling coals over to a spot under the shade trees. Joe and I built the coals up while Lucy and Mama finished cleaning the Gar. When the coals were ready, we wrapped the Gar in fresh, green palmetto branches and placed them on the gray coals. While the fish was cooking, Joe and I started working on our chores.

After we loaded the wagon down with firewood and moved it to the cabins, we unhitched the mules from the wagon and fed and watered the horses. Also, we brought the water buckets up to the porch so Mama and my grandmother could wash the few clothes that we had. After that, we went and sat down beside the fire and enjoyed the smell of the cooking fish.

To my surprise, Lucy came out with some hardtack that she had made on a wood burning stove in her cabin. Together, we all sat around the fire and enjoyed the fish and hardtack. Even Grandma decided to try it, and although I imagine she was starving, she did not have a look of approval on her face. She had been pampered by James for so many years, and I don't think she could bring herself low enough to enjoy it with the rest of us. The transition that we were making seemed to be the toughest on her.

After we finished eating, Lucy, Joe, and I took what was left of the fish and cut it into small strips. We took at least ten pounds of fresh white meat and hung it in the old smoke house behind the cabins. Joe and I took some of the pecan wood that had been stacked behind the house and cut it into smaller pieces. We fed the pecan into the smokehouse with the hot coals we had leftover to begin smoking the fish. I knew we had to have something to sustain us until Pa came home.

Over the next two days, it seemed like everyone was going through the motions to pass the time. We were eagerly awaiting Pa's return, and I caught myself looking down the long road multiple times, hoping to see his horse. Other than two rabbits that I killed with Pa's shotgun, we mainly lived off of hardtack and smoked fish. By the end of the third day, Lucy had run out of wheat and flour, and the thought of fish was repulsive to me. I was growing impatient, along with everyone else. I couldn't understand what could be taking Pa so long to return.

On the fourth day, Grandma began to complain much more about how she was "famished." Joe and I didn't know what that meant, but we would look at each other and smile every time she went on a rant. Lucy and Mama told us to stop laughing and cutting up, but we couldn't help ourselves. The only peace and joy that I had been feeling was when Joe and I would laugh and joke together.

The truth is, I was beginning to admire Joe and his character. He was fierce and strong, but he was also humble and soft spoken. We were getting to know each other in those first days, and we began to form a friendship like I had never known. We didn't ask to experience any of the things that we did, but the Bible says, *"My brethren, count it all joy when ye fall into divers temptations; Knowing this, that the trying of your faith worketh patience. But let patience have her perfect work, that ye may be perfect and entire, wanting nothing."*

10

REBUILDING

Early the next morning, I was dreaming that I heard the unmistakable sound of a horse approaching. I could see the hooves of the horse pounding the sandy road beneath them. I could not see the face of the dark rider in my dream, but what once seemed to be a distant sound became much closer. Then everything became silent.

The sound of boots coming across the wooden porch suddenly woke me from a deep sleep. Whoever was approaching the door to the cabin was closing the distance fast. I sprang up from the bed, grabbed my pistol, and ran to the doorway. When the door opened, I drew a bead on the face of my father. "Pa! You're home!"

"Dadgum it, boy! I ain't had a pistol in my face in a long time. I oughta tan your hide!" he joked.

Pa grabbed me, hugged me, and pulled me in close. "Boy, we are gonna be alright. Your Grandpa Lewis will be here shortly, and he hired a crew to help us build a new home." I knew Pa would figure something out! I also became increasingly thankful for the deep pockets of my grandpa Lewis.

Lewis had recently built a church for my father, not far from our property. I imagined he would use the same crew to travel down from Montgomery and help us with our new home. Grandpa Lewis was a builder himself, and he was well known in town for erecting the Dexter House and many others. None of us knew where he had gotten his money, but there were tales of "old silver" making the trip from Maine to Alabama with him in eighteen thirty.

When it came to Grandpa Lewis, I didn't ask too many questions. He was an enterprising man, but also a man who drew a person in with his character and personality. He treated us better than he had to during those times, and we would not have made it without him. He often reminded us that the Harrisons descended from Benjamin Harrison, one of the signers of the Declaration of Independence. I always thought he was joking, but Pa swore it to be true.

His wife Jane came from a very well-known, prominent family from Georgia. Grandma Jane's father owned The Pantheon plantation which was located about five miles from us. While her father ran the plantation, Jane preferred to live in her and Grandpa Lewis's home in Montgomery. Coming from a rich family, she, along with Grandma Elizabeth, appreciated the finer things in life. Grandpa Lewis often came and stayed on the farm while she stayed in town. It seemed as if they needed a break from each other at certain times of the year, and it was mainly during planting season.

On what became Mason Road, there were the Smith, Mason, Harrison and Owen families. My pa, Doc Harrison, had met my mother, Mary "Molly" Watkins Smith, and they fell in love and got married. Grandpa Lewis was already a very influential man, but when he married Grandma Jane, it seemed as if our families owned every square inch of land for miles. What obviously set my immediate family apart at that time was the fact that we did not support slavery and secession, yet every day we seemed to be surrounded by it.

I asked Pa how he knew which cabin I was in, and he said, "I figured you would get tired of sleeping on that floor in there with your mama, and your horse is tied up right there, son." I smiled and nodded as I had to admit to myself that my father was always a step ahead of me. We often silently acknowledged the fact that he was much wiser than I. Afterward, we would smile and move on, and thankfully, he never rubbed it in.

Later that morning, I became excited when I heard wagons coming down the road. From a distance of roughly one hundred yards, I could see Grandpa Lewis in the first wagon raising his hand to greet us. Behind him were at least a dozen men riding ten wagons that seemed to keep coming and coming. Each wagon was being pulled by two mules, and each was loaded down with lumber.

Mama and Grandma Elizabeth must have heard the commotion because they came out to greet the wagons along with Lucy, Nan, and Joe. As Lucy led her children out into the yard, I noticed something was different about her. Mama, who was petite and quite literally the same size as Lucy, had given her one of her clean dresses. Lucy was a beautiful woman, and although I was only thirteen, I could see that. I reckon that's why Joe was so protective of her and also why Grandpa James had so many problems with the men chasing after her.

As Joe approached, I hit him on the arm and asked, "Were you gonna sleep all day?"

"I might have if y'all had let me." We both laughed and made our way over to the wagons behind Pa. I was anxious to see Grandpa Lewis for the first time in a while. I loved spending time with him and hearing him tell stories of the old days in Wiscasset, Maine, and Montgomery.

My favorite stories were when he would talk about his whaling voyages as a young man. His first sailing trip was around the Horn in a ship called Martha. The captain of the Essex, George Pollard from Herman Melville's *Moby Dick,* was rescued by my grandpa and his crew after his second accident at sea. Pollard's sailing career unfortunately came to an end at that point, but Lewis always talked about how lucky they were to make it back alive. All in all, my grandpa was an older man, but he still demanded respect, and the stories and exploits from his earlier days proved that.

As Pa approached Lewis, he asked, "How was the trip?"

Grandpa Lewis replied, "Slow and bumpy, but we made it in one piece." Then I noticed him staring at the remains of the old homesite as he tried to hide the fact that he was visibly shaken. "Take me to the cemetery immediately! I must see where they are buried." Pa agreed and told Joe and me to bring the horses.

When Joe and I walked the horses around the front, Grandpa asked, "Where is Achilles?"

I hesitantly replied, "Grandpa, the Yanks took your horse with just about everything else. We found these horses in the old cotton barn in the back."

A look of disgust came across his face, and he asked, "Can that Wilson boy show no restraint on this pointless endeavor?" Pa then confirmed that he had received news downtown that it was Captain James Wilson's troops that burned our homes.

"The war is all but over! What business do they have coming through here and harming innocent civilians and their properties? Come, let's ride," he said as he mounted the front horse. Grandpa was still in good shape for his age and was a master horseman. He was of average height and stout, just like the rest of us. Joe and I were both blown away when he mounted the horse as if he were our age.

Pa, Joe, and I fell in behind Grandpa and made our way to the pecan grove where the bodies of my brother Mason and Grandfather Smith lay. When we made it to the spot where the fresh dirt was still visible, we dismounted and approached the graves. "Could you not have waited to let me say goodbye to each of them, son?" Grandpa asked.

"You know that we have talked about this, and time was not in our favor. We did what we had to do," Pa replied.

"I understand, but that makes this no easier," Lewis said.

Just then, with tears rolling down his face, Grandpa looked up and locked eyes with Joe. "Who is this boy?"

Before Pa could speak up, I said, "He is a part of our family now, along with his mama and sister."

"What do you mean they are a part of our family?"

"Lucy was one of Grandma Elizabeth's servants, and this is her son, Joe. He has a sister named Nan. They were the only servants left, and they saved Grandma Elizabeth's life."

Grandpa looked at Doc, and when Pa nodded his head in agreement, Lewis said, "Well, let it be so."

Grandpa changed the subject quickly, and it was as if we were supposed to ignore what had just taken place. Two families came together that morning in a pecan grove amidst terrible times and tragedy. Pa and I already considered Joe to be family, but when Grandpa Lewis agreed, it seemed to be confirmation for all of us. I learned something that morning about my Pa and Grandpa. Not every white man was racist, and it was their mutual understanding of their relationships with Christ that set them apart. Joe wasn't just a piece of property to them; he was seen as a fellow child of God.

The Bible said that a lamp on a hill cannot be hidden, and that proved itself to be true that morning. It didn't matter what the world around us looked like because we trusted that God's word was the final truth. I gained a brother that morning, and although Joe didn't take to it as quickly as I did, I understood why. I had seen the mistreatment of slaves, and in that moment, what I felt for Joe was love, respect, understanding, and sorrow. But what impressed me the most was the fact that he seemed to be undaunted by it all. He was brave enough to stand among men whom he once thought he had to fear.

Joe learned that day that he was not dealing with the average white man and that he could be proud to stand alongside us because we didn't think twice about accepting his presence. We earned each other's loyalty in those days. Thankfully, Pa was a praying man, and God saw us through those days after we lost our home. It was the hardest time that I had seen in my short life, but some extraordinary relationships came out of those hard times. I believe we all learned to respect each other in different ways because we all had to pull our own weight.

Before we left the cemetery, I heard Grandpa explaining to Pa why Grandma Jane didn't make the trip. He said she claimed that she couldn't handle seeing the aftermath. Lewis offered to take Mama, Elizabeth, Lucy and Nan back to town with him so that Jane could take them shopping and pamper them. Pa said, "That'll be up to them, Dad. We have a house to build, and we've got the rations and supplies to work until it's time to go back to town for more. They do need clothes and more supplies, though, so if they agree, I'd be much obliged." Grandpa agreed, and we made our way back to the homesite.

The ladies could hardly contain their excitement when they got the invitation to go stay with Grandma Jane in town. She had all of the luxuries that most couldn't afford at the time, so I imagined it would be a special experience for them all. Grandma Elizabeth seemed to be the happiest, as she and Jane had a history of gossiping and living a more lavish lifestyle together. Those days were over for the most part, and hard work became the fuel that moved our family along after the war.

Mama and Elizabeth had to convince Lucy to leave Joe with us. Pa tried to explain to me the pain she must have felt when Joe's daddy was sold to another slaver. Pa told me that Joe was just a little boy and Nan was a baby when James sold Joe's father to a man from Louisiana. That might have been why Lucy stayed around to watch the Yanks murder him in his own yard. The truth is, none of us saw eye to eye with Grandpa James and the way he treated his servants, so I completely understood why Lucy was hesitant about leaving Joe with us at that time.

"What was his name, Joe's daddy?" I asked.

"If I remember correctly, I believe his name was Levy, and I'm sure he was a fine man. James allowed Mr. Pierce to go too far once Levy became defiant. Your grandfather was a prideful man, Pat. Instead of punishing Levy, he decided to sell him for a pretty penny after he put a beating on Pierce in front of everyone." I felt nothing but sorrow as I watched Joe urge his crying mother to join the others on the wagon.

Once we got Lucy on Grandpa's wagon, Pa began to give orders to the men who were standing around. There were a dozen good men there, but Grandpa explained to Pa that he would be taking two men back to Montgomery with him. Pa said, "You know we need every hand we can get out here."

Grandpa replied, "Well, we would like to make it back to Montgomery alive, and these two fine young men from Plantersville know their way around a rifle. I'm getting too old to fight anymore, son. Now, what if the wrong posse rides up on an old man with a wagon full of white ladies and two colored girls?" Pa didn't have much of a reply for him, and before they rode off, we said our goodbyes.

The men who had been unloading the wagons all morning began to come up and introduce themselves to Pa. The foreman was a short, well-dressed man named Isham Stubbs from Montgomery, and the other younger man from Autauga County went by the name of Jacob House. He seemed to be in charge of the rest of the crew, as Mr. Stubbs was the brains of the operation. The rest of the crew were men that Grandpa trusted and had been under Mr. Stubbs since he began working for Grandpa.

Joe and I sat together and watched in amazement as the crew began to work together. Pa looked over at us and said, "I know you two boys don't think you're about to sit around and watch us do all of the work." Joe and I quickly jumped up and walked over to Pa. Before Pa could give us our orders, I begged him to walk away from the crew so that I could tell him something. Shaking his head, he walked over and asked me what was so important. I think Joe knew what I was about to tell him, but I called him over anyway, so that he could help me convince Pa of the truth.

"Pa, two men from the McCrae plantation came across the creek with their hounds and held Mama, Grandma, Lucy, Nan, and Joe at gunpoint," I said.

Pa's face began to turn red. "Where were you and what happened?" I continued by telling him how I drew my pistol on them and that they were looking for runaway slaves. I told him that I was confident that if I hadn't been armed that they would have taken Lucy, Nan, and Joe. Pa looked at Joe, and Joe nodded his head to confirm. "Well, it sounds like we need to make a trip over to Angus McCrae's place before this gets out of hand."

11

ANGUS McCRAE

After Pa told the crew that we would return before dark, he told Joe and me to mount up and follow him. Pa seemed to be determined and wasn't saying much, so Joe and I didn't ask any questions. We struggled to keep up as we left the new home site and rode hard down between the oaks that lined the road. Instead of turning to the right toward the McCrae plantation, Pa turned left and rode toward our old home site on the hill. I turned to look at Joe as he rode up beside me, and he looked as confused as I was.

Pa was already dismounting his horse before Joe and I rode up to the old barn. He motioned for us to stay where we were, and he disappeared around the right side of the barn. "What's your Pa doing, Pat?" Joe asked.

"I don't know, but judging by the look on his face, he means business." I hadn't ever known Pa to be short-tempered, but after I told him about the overseers coming across the creek, he seemed to be wasting no time.

As I sat there deep in thought, Joe spoke up. "Pat, I've got to tell you somethin'."

"Oh yeah, what's that?"

"You know that big man at the creek? Well, he used to work for your grandpa Smith, and we had some bad dealings with him. That man is the reason Mr. Smith sold my daddy." I selfishly wished I had pulled the trigger on Pierce when I had the chance.

"So, you know that man?"

"Yeah, he was the one who used to beat and rape my mama, and when Daddy finally caught him, he went crazy."

"What happened?"

"Well, Daddy put a pretty good beating on him, and when Mr. Smith found out, he sold Pierce and my pop to a man from Louisiana. Or at least that is what we were told."

No wonder Lucy and Nan were so shaken up earlier. What Joe had just told me was a quick reminder that what we had just been through paled in comparison to what Joe's family had experienced. Just as I started to tell Joe how sorry I was, Pa walked around the corner carrying three rifles.

"What? You didn't think I was going to let those Yanks have our guns, too did you?" he asked.

Smiling, I said, "No, sir." He then brought two lever-action rifles and placed one across each of our laps and said, "They are loaded."

Joe said, "Now, hold on a minute, Pastor Doc. I ain't ever shot a gun before."

Then Pa mounted his horse and said, "Hopefully you won't have to learn today. We'd better go if we are going to reach the McCrae plantation and make it back before dark." Joe and I were both confused and hesitant, but we had no choice but to follow when Pa rode off in a hurry.

The McCrae plantation reached the back of Grandpa James's property, but it was still close to four miles to his main house if we took the road. We tried our best to keep up with Pa and hang on to the rifles at the same time. We weren't as experienced as Pa on horseback, but we reached the McCrae house in about thirty minutes. Before we came to the opening between the two huge pillars leading into their property, Pa stopped and waited for us. We still had a couple of hours before dark, but for some reason, I felt rushed and uneasy.

There was a large arch over the driveway between the two stone pillars. At the top and in the middle, it read *McCrae*. "This man must be rich like your granddaddy was, Pat," Joe said.

Pa chimed in and said, "He's got just as much or more money than James, but a lot of what he possesses hasn't been earned honestly." Everybody knew the McCraes were crooked and cruel. For that reason, I couldn't help but wonder why Pa was planning on riding up with just the three of us. He always claimed that he feared no man, only God. I guess that was his opportunity to walk it out.

The driveway seemed to go on forever as we went from a trot to a walk. Both sides of the road were planted in cotton as far as we could see. The tiny seedlings were just beginning to poke through the soil. We passed rows and rows until we came to an oak grove and a bend in the road. When we came around the turn under the massive oak trees, we saw the McCrae house situated in the middle of the grove.

The servants' cabins lined the right side of the road, but there was no sign of anyone. It was eerily quiet, and as we approached, Pa motioned for us to ride up closer. Both Joe and I were lost in the moment, and I imagine he was questioning the situation as well. I admired his courage for riding with us to an unknown place on a horse he had barely ridden while carrying a gun he had never fired. I'm glad he was brave because that was our only option as we approached the huge, white home that stood before us.

Pa rode up to the first of the individually spaced, bronze colored hitching posts. They were adorned with the heads of horses on the tops, and I had never seen anything like it. Joe and I cautiously tied our horses off as Pa began walking towards the front door of the house. By the time we had reached the front porch, Pa had already knocked on the huge wooden door.

It wasn't long before we could hear footsteps rapidly approaching the front door. When the door opened, a small, colored girl who I imagine was around the age of sixteen said, "Yes, sir, can I help you?"

"Yes, ma'am. I am looking for Mr. Angus McCrae. I have urgent business with him."

"One minute," she replied. Then she quietly shut the front door and walked away.

As we stood outside and waited, I asked Pa what he intended to say to Mr. McCrae. "Son, why don't you let me handle this? I know exactly what I'm going to do, and that is find out why his overseers held my family at gunpoint. Do you have a better idea?" I just stood there and sort of smirked at Joe as we both realized Pa had put me in my place.

After a few minutes had gone by, we heard the girl coming back, and Pa said, " Alright, y'all let me do the talking and don't speak unless you are spoken to."

We both nodded in agreement as she opened the massive front door. "You can come on in. Mr. McCrae is straight up those stairs to his office. He is expecting you."

The interior of the house was like nothing I had ever seen. Bellewood was nice, but it was nothing like this. There was fine art on each wall and expensive things that we had never seen. There were deer, wild hogs, and foreign animals mounted all around us. Oddly, it was so quiet in the large house that we could have heard a pin drop.

After we had taken in our surroundings for a brief moment, we began to make our way to the stairs that split the room down the middle. Pa went first, followed by me, and Joe was last. When I got close to the top of the stairs, I heard a voice up ahead, but could not see the man.

"How ya doing, Angus?" Pa asked. When I finally saw the man that I had been picturing in my mind, there were no similarities.

The man who stood before us was an older man with neatly combed white hair. He was slightly overweight, and it seemed that he relied on a cane to hold himself up. I reckon I was expecting to see a much younger and stronger man. Just when I became curious about the patch over his left eye, he asked, "What's the matter, boy? You've never seen somebody with one eye before?"

It seemed as if McCrae was testing my character right from the start. I confidently replied, "Yes, sir, my uncle lost his eye at the Battle of Seven Pines. I reckon I was just curious how you lost yours." Then the old man asked us to sit down as he walked in our direction from the window overlooking the grounds behind his home. Joe and I sat down in the chairs in front of McCrae's desk, but Pa never sat.

McCrea slowly made his way around to our left with his eyes fixed on Joe. "So, what brings you out this way, Doc? It has been a while since I have seen you."

"You may want to sit down for this one, Angus. This is a serious matter."

"Oh, I assure you, there is nothing so serious that I don't already know about it. I imagine you are talking about Mr. Pierce's little run-in with your son down at the creek."

"Yes. I am glad you already know. By the way, is Pierce around here today?" Pa asked.

"Oh, no. He is out handling some business for me at the moment. I can relay a message to him if you would like," the old man smirked.

"Well, you can tell him not to cross that creek again because if he does, I will have him arrested."

McCrae began to laugh, "There is no law around here, Doc. If you want to do something, then you have to do it yourself. I will surely relay the message to Pierce, but I can not guarantee that he will listen. He is a rebellious man, unfortunately, but he is a good, firm overseer. You should recognize him. He used to work for James at Bellewood."

"I know who he is. You tell him to stay away from my family and that property back there. I'm serious, Angus."

The old man, hesitating, said, "You have my word." Then walking closer to Joe, he asked, "The negro boy that Pierce said was with your boy at the creek was about the age of this boy here. Was he not?" Angus suddenly reached over and ripped Joe's shirt at the shoulder, exposing his arm. I sprang from my seat grabbed McCrae's arm, and warned him to back up. "Easy, son, I just wanted to see who this boy belonged to. The boy looks familiar, is all."

"I can assure you that he doesn't carry your brand," Pa said. "This boy and his mother saved Elizabeth's life, and as far as I'm concerned, he is under my protection now."

Angus began to laugh hysterically and said, "I heard the Yanks burned Bellewood to the ground. I saw the smoke myself. Lewis didn't have enough silver to buy them off? It seemed that Captain Wilson may have preferred gold over silver."

Pa replied, "I should have known you paid them off to save your own hide. It looks as if you have lost all of your servants, though."

Angus replied, "It seems one of the nigger men led an escape while we were occupied with the Yanks. We will find them in due time. We will find them all."

"Angus, I can't tell you what to do on your own property, but you just make sure that none of your business comes across that creek. You leave my family out of this!"

Angus nodded his head in agreement. "If our business here is finished, you can ask Fannie Mae to show you out." As we began to walk out of the room, I looked at Angus, and he gave me a wink with a smirk on his face.

Once we got into the hallway, Joe whispered, "Something ain't right about that man." I could feel the tension that had been building up in my body subside as we walked back down the stairs and out the front door.

As we approached our horses, Pa said, "You see, boys, there is always a way to handle a bad situation without violence and conflict." While I believed what Pa was saying, I still had an uneasy feeling that the issue was not resolved. Joe tore his shirt sleeve off, then ripped off the other one.

When I looked at him like he was crazy, he said, "Ain't no need in having a shirt with a big hole in it." Laughing, I agreed as we mounted our horses and began to make our way back down the driveway.

Before we had made it very far, we heard screaming coming from behind the main house. Pa urged us to ignore the screams and follow him, but I couldn't just ride away. I turned my horse around as Pa was yelling at me to stop. For some reason, his commands were falling short. I just had to go back there. Joe followed behind me, and as we came around the corner of the house, I suddenly wished I had listened to Pa.

There was a colored man tied to a whipping post, and he could barely hold himself up. Three of McCrae's men were standing around him and shouting profanities. A woman and two children, a boy and a girl, were sitting off to the side and being forced to watch. I recognized one of the men to be the redheaded younger man from the creek. He seemed to be enjoying himself as they mocked the man and spat in his face.

The hatred I felt building up in my heart for those men would fuel the misguided decisions that I would soon make. I could feel the adrenaline pumping through my body when Pa rode up beside us. The men turned to see us watching and began to walk our way.

Pa shouted, "Come on, boys! I mean it!"

When I saw the look on Joe's face, I snapped back into reality and said, "Come on, Joe, let's go." Then we rode hard toward the new homesite to make it back before dark.

When we arrived, I noticed that the crew had made a good deal of progress on the foundation. They seemed to be winding down as the day was coming to an end. After we dismounted, Mr. Stubbs came over and assured Pa that the crew had gotten off to a good start. He said they would resume their work at daylight, and he talked of the goals that he had for the next day. I could see that Joe was still bothered by what we had just witnessed, and I went to sit down beside him.

"You alright, Joe?"

"I've seen it all of my life, Pat. There's got to be a day coming when all of this will end."

"That day is coming, Joe. You're free now, and things are going to change. We're gonna make dang sure of it." It didn't seem that my words held much weight with Joe, but I had every intention of keeping my word and making him feel welcome and equal to the rest of us. "Come on, let's go sit by the fire," I said.

The men had built a small fire off to the side of the foundation, so Joe and I went over and joined them. The men in the crew were engaged in a deep conversation with Pa for quite some time. Joe and I kicked back and listened to the conversations go on and on. When Pa decided it was time to call it a night, I called him over. "Hey, Pa, you remember me telling you about that gobbler Joe and I found down at the creek?"

"Yeah. Are you and Joe wanting to go hunt him?"

I excitedly nodded my head, and Pa grinned from ear to ear. "We can go down there at daylight, but we need to be back here early to get started on the house." I was overwhelmed with excitement as we went to our cabin for the night. Joe and I lay in the dark, and I tried my best to explain to Joe what we could possibly experience the next morning.

12

DISCOVERING OLOMILL

All night, I tossed and turned on the hard, thin mattress. I was haunted by dreams and visions of the man being beaten by McCrae's men. I could hear the mother and daughter crying and the man desperately begging for his life. I woke up time and time again, sweating and attempting to pray the horrible dreams away. I feared falling back to sleep would only bring the dreams back, but I knew I needed rest if I would be of any value on the upcoming hunt.

I had finally fallen into a deep sleep when Pa woke me up and said, "Come on, boy. You'd better get up if we are going hunting this morning."

"Pa, I had nightmares all night. I barely slept a wink."

"Well, we can go hunting another morning if you want."

"No, no I will be fine," I assured him. It didn't matter how I felt. I was not missing that hunt for the world. I reckon Joe slept like a baby because he never made a noise until I shook him.

"Are we going hunting?" he asked.

"Yep, Pa's got the scatter gun, and he is waiting for us outside." Joe and I got dressed and stepped outside to discover a beautiful, crisp morning.

There was almost no wind, and we could hear for a long way. Pa brought the lantern and the shotgun, then the three of us tiptoed through the whiskey bottles and passed out workers.

We hit the old roadbed behind the homesite, relying on the lantern to guide our way. It wasn't until we had broken away from the workers' fire that I realized how dark it still was. Pa always said that men liked to act tough, but there was nothing wrong with having a chill run down your spine in the dark. That familiar feeling was beginning to come over me as we ventured further and further into the darkness.

I began to remind myself that there was nothing in those woods that could stand up to Pa's scatter gun. Joe stayed right on my heels as I stayed right on Pa's. While I was edgy about having such a long walk in the dark, I was relieved to know that we would have plenty of time to get close to the gobbler before daylight. Pa had always taught me to get as close as I could to the turkeys in the dark so that we would be amongst them once the sun came up. Then, hopefully, they would fly down from their roosts and be close enough for the old scatter gun.

All of a sudden, Pa stopped, and I ran into his back as Joe ran into mine. I imagine we looked like cattle being herded through a narrow chute, but walking in the dark will do crazy things to your eyes. Pa laughed and said, " All right, boys. The creek is just ahead. Pat, you know where we are going, so you lead the way." I was caught off guard and felt the weight of the morning fall upon my shoulders.

Pa snuffed the lantern out and set it at the base of a big tree. The entire world around us became black. There was not yet enough light to see where we were walking, so I knew we had to take it one step at a time. Each step was a step closer to resting our bottoms at the base of a tree for the rest of the morning. Cautiously, we began to navigate down the edge of the creek toward the turkey roost.

We moved so slowly that I could feel each stick beneath my feet. As we attempted to avoid breaking the sticks, Pa whispered, "Walk heel to toe." The trees were nothing more than black masses in front of us. The sound of the creek water slowly running beside me and a clean area to place my foot were my only guides. Each noise we made could possibly alert the turkeys and give away our location.

In a straight line, the turkeys were not that far from us, but we were forced to follow the bends and curves of the creek. Once we made it around the first bend, my eyes began to adjust, and navigating the gnarly woods became much easier. I tried to remember how far down the creek the turkeys were, but it seemed impossible to do in the thick woods. Everything around us looked the same. I stopped briefly and quietly asked Joe, "How much further do you think they were?"

"We've got to be getting close," he whispered.

We continued on, fighting the thick underbrush while trying to remain as quiet as possible. After walking a good distance, we came into an opening, and I stopped. When Pa and Joe made it to my side, I whispered, "I think this is the spot they were roosted in."

"I don't doubt it, son. There are some pretty hardwoods back here," Pa said, studying the ground. "There is plenty of fresh scratching in these leaves. We need to sit down right here for a while and listen."

Earlier, it seemed as if the woods were quiet, but now I was picking up on every little sound. Among the critters were frogs, hoot owls, an occasional songbird, and the unmistakable sound of the whippoorwill. Although I had worked up a sweat, I seemed to be settling in now and cooling off. Joe was seated to my right and Pa to my left at the base of a shagbark. The sounds of the woods around me provided instant peace as I let out a deep sigh of relief and began to close my eyes.

I began to drift off when I suddenly heard what we came to hear. The old gobbler had given up his location, and he did it earlier than usual too. We all jumped up, and Pa said, "He sounds to be a couple of hundred yards down and across the creek." My heart sank as I realized we wouldn't be able to cross the creek and hunt him on the McCrae's land. Then my spirits lifted as Pa said, "Come on, we can still try to call him across the creek."

Before we started walking, I looked at Joe and asked, "Did you hear him?"

"What do you mean, did I hear him? You'd have to be deaf not to hear that. What are we gonna do now?"

Smiling, I said, "We are gonna go to him!" It was amazing how that one turkey gobble woke me up, and I quickly forgot about my sleepless night. I now had all of the energy I needed as Joe and I fell in behind Pa.

We eased down toward the creek and in the direction of the gobble. We moved quickly at first, but once we had made it about one hundred yards, Pa stopped. We sat there and listened as the day began to wake up around us. Shortly after, the turkey gobbled again, and it sounded much closer. Pa smiled, "He ain't far."

We quietly crept up the hill and turned toward the turkey. We made it another forty yards or so when Pa stopped again. "Did y'all hear that?" he asked.

We both whispered, "No."

"Shh, listen!" A few moments later, a hen turkey quietly tree yelped above us. Then, multiple hens started responding to each other. "Y'all find a tree and sit down. His hens are on this side of the creek with us," Pa said.

Joe and I slowly walked backward to a red oak and sat down beside each other. Pa crawled over to us and said, "I'm going to ease back behind y'all. Pat, take the gun. This bird is yours. Y'all be still and don't move unless it's your trigger finger." Then Pa disappeared behind us, and I rested the gun on my knee.

The hens above us continued to softly yelp as we listened to Pa slowly moving through the leaves behind us. One of the hens then began to "cut" excitedly, and the tom responded by gobbling. "He is close!" Joe said.

"He is roosted on McCrae's side, but if all of his hens are on this side, then we may have a chance of him flying down over here." It was still early and fairly dark, so we leaned back and enjoyed the show.

Every time a crow or a hoot owl made their presence known, the old tom would fire off and gobble back. He had no clue we were there to interrupt his morning ritual as he continued to gobble. At one point, he gobbled so many times without ceasing that it sounded like he ran out of air and choked himself. Their morning dance had never been witnessed by anyone outside of that creek bottom until that morning. We were fortunate enough to be the only spectators present.

As I looked up to thank God for that experience, I noticed Joe also seemed to be lost in the moment. Immediately, I knew that we were right where we were supposed to be. Something just felt right. Everything that we had been through seemed to take a back seat to the entertainment in front of us. There was no question in my mind that God placed us in a particular place that morning to carry out his plans.

Lost in the moment, Joe and I both jumped when a second gobbler made his presence known. This bird was much closer and had been tight-lipped all morning. The original turkey was still gobbling in the tree, but he was across the creek. So, I decided we'd better shift our attention to the turkey that was on our property and much closer to us.

The sun began to peak over the trees and provide a warmth that calmed me, and I stopped shaking. I'm not sure if I was cold or nervous, but I imagine it was a mixture of both. I knew the turkeys would soon fly down from their limbs and the hunt would be on. Joe and I decided to shift around the oak to our right and toward the second gobbler. The only thing left for them to do was fly down.

Pa began to softly call behind us, and Joe gave me a look that suggested he was impressed with how realistic Pa's calling sounded. I reckon it was nothing new to me because I had heard him do it since I had ears to hear. He was truly a master woodsman and could mimic a hen turkey like no one I had ever heard. I was confident from a young age that I had the best teacher when it came to hunting. There weren't as many turkeys around in those days, but when we did run into one, I rarely saw a tom get the best of Pa.

When the second gobbler heard Pa softly yelping, he immediately responded by gobbling. Joe slowly leaned over and said, "He sounds a lot closer than he did a few minutes ago."

"He turned his attention to us and spun around on the limb. That is why he sounds closer," I explained. As the bird acknowledged our presence, I began to see if I could spot him on the limb. Every time he gobbled, the other turkey responded, and I knew we were in for a show.

The later it got, the better I could see through the thick foliage into the treetops. Finally, the next time that he gobbled, I caught movement. The bird was much closer than I had anticipated. "There he is, I see him."

"Where? I don't see him," Joe asked.

Now I could see the gobbler clearly as he went in and out of strut. I had learned that "strutting" was when a gobbler puffed his feathers out to show off for the ladies. What was a tall, slender bird would become a round ball of beautiful feathers that would mesmerize any artist. Pa's calling seemed to be working as the fired-up gobbler continued to gobble. He began to walk back and forth on the limb, bobbing his head to see if he could locate the hen or potentially find a landing spot.

"I see him, I see him," Joe whispered. I watched as Joe fell under the same trance that I fell under the first time I saw a tom. What seemed like a mythical creature quickly became very real. I positioned the double-barreled shotgun on my left knee and slowly cocked both hammers. When Joe heard the hammers click, he asked, "Pat, you about to shoot?"

I whispered, "No, but I want to be ready in case he flies down toward us."

Suddenly, I heard wings flapping to my left, and when I turned my head, I saw a hen land within twenty yards. "Don't move. There is a turkey on the ground right beside us," I whispered to Joe. Then the hens that were roosting above us and in front of us began to fly down. They communicated with the gobbler by doing an excited call known as the fly-down cackle.

Within seconds, there were eight hens grouped together in the hardwoods. They began chasing each other around and yelping loudly. The hen to our left was making her way to the flock when I saw the gobbler pitch down to our right. He didn't fly down like the rest of the turkeys. He silently pitched straight to the ground and began making his way to the hens. What we witnessed next, I will never forget.

The lone gobbler that was roosting across the creek hadn't made a noise in quite some time. That all changed when he heard the other turkey gobble on the ground. He gobbled one last time on the limb to announce his descent, then down he came with his wings locked, and I admired his beauty as he coasted through the treetops. When he finally landed among the other turkeys, he was face-to-face with the other gobbler. They may have been friends the day before, but that morning they acted as if they were bitter rivals.

The two big toms circled each other, standing fully erect, one waiting for the other to make the first move. "Are you seeing this?" I asked Joe.

"Yeah."

I should have known he was locked in when I saw his legs shaking as badly as mine were. The two gobblers began to aggressively beat each other with their wings, and the fight was on.

They attempted to peck each other's eyes out and beat the other into submission. Their heads were bright red as if they were covered in blood. The fight went on for what seemed like forever. The fight was so intense that when the hens began to walk off, the gobblers didn't notice their departure. It was time to seize what may be our only opportunity.

I realized Pa and I were on the same page when he began to call loudly and aggressively behind us. The two toms separated for the first time and checked their surroundings. With their necks fully extended, their eyes searched the hardwoods for what they had been fighting over. Pa let out a few soft clucks, and that is all it took.

The noticeably larger bird gobbled and began to run in our direction with his competition close behind. "Here we go!" I shouldered the gun tightly. Looking down between the double barrels, all I could see were two red heads bobbing up and down. I feared they were going to run us over before I could settle the bead on the larger turkey's head. Just then, Pa called one last time, and the two gobblers stopped, extended their necks, and presented me with a shot.

My heart was pounding in my chest so loud that I could hear it beating. If it wasn't mine, I'm certain it was Joe's that I heard. I heard Pa behind me whispering, "Shoot him!" The bead at the end of the shotgun's barrel was moving more than I'd like to admit. When it finally settled between the turkey's neck and the feather line, I squeezed the trigger.

The shotgun blast silenced the woods for a moment. As the smoke cleared, I could hear the undeniable sound of a turkey flopping in the leaves. The other gobbler, not knowing what happened, seized his opportunity. He began whipping the turkey that I shot and gobbling so close that it rattled my chest. I handed the shotgun to Joe and said, "Put the bead on his head and pull the front trigger." He quickly grabbed it from my hands and began to take aim.

While the gobbler was attacking his old rival and asserting his dominance, Joe effortlessly sent him to meet his maker. We had fired twice and killed two gobblers! It was a true double if I'd ever seen one! Pa ran up and excitedly said, "Go get your birds boys!" Joe dropped the gun in the leaves, and we took off. We didn't have a long run, but by the time we got there, we didn't know which turkey was which.

Pa said, "Aw, it doesn't matter! Y'all grab those birds by the head." With their wings still flapping, Joe and I hoisted our prizes as Pa looked on. We both took a pretty good beating there for a minute, but it was worth it. I was laughing hysterically at Joe, and he was laughing right along with me. After a few moments of chaos, the two birds took their last breaths.

"Boys, I hope y'all appreciate what just happened," Pa said. "I have been turkey hunting my entire life, and I don't believe I have ever seen anything like that." Then he told Joe and me to bring our gobblers down to the creek. "If y'all are going to kill them, then you are going to learn how to clean them." Joe and I both looked at each other, laughed and threw the turkeys over our shoulders.

The water was about ankle deep where Pa led us down. I recognized the beautiful spot as not being too far from where Joe and I caught the huge alligator gar. Steam slowly rose from the surface of the water toward the warm sun as Pa shouted, "Look at this beautiful setting the Lord has provided this morning, boys!" All I remember feeling in that moment was gratitude until our peaceful moment of reflection was quickly interrupted.

Suddenly, something began crashing through the tall, green palmettos. I scrambled back towards the gun that we had left on the creek bank. By the time I reached my gun, Pa called me off and said, "Pat, leave it!" When

I looked down the creek, I saw a colored man running in the opposite direction. Pa began shouting for the man to stop, but he kept running like his life depended on it.

"Y'all just gonna let him run off?" Pa sarcastically asked. Before I could reply, Joe and I made eye contact, and we took off down the creek. I could feel my toes gripping the sand as we blew through the ankle-deep water. My adrenaline took over, and I became focused on the task at hand. Fortunately, the steep bank on the right side of the creek formed a wall, trapping the stranger. Once we realized that he had nowhere to go, it turned into an old-fashioned foot race.

I had been told all my life that I was "fast for a white boy," but I was humbled that morning when Joe showed me what true speed looked like. His legs were pulling so hard that he began to sling sand in my eyes as he pulled away from me. In my entire life, I had never seen anyone run like that. Joe's slender build and long legs hinted at the fact that he would be fast. Before I knew it, Joe had caught up with the man who was trying to climb the bank to safety.

Joe reached up and grabbed the man's feet and pulled him back down the bank. "Hold him right there, Joe," I said. By the time Joe got his hands on the man, I jumped in and we both held him face down until Pa finally walked up.

Pa jokingly said, "Joe, I believe you may be half man and half deer."

"Quit fightin'!" Joe yelled as the man struggled to break free from our grip.

"Well, what do we have here? We just wanted to ask you why you were trespassing. You didn't have to run off on us." The man tried to speak, but his voice was muffled due to Joe and me holding his face in the sand. Pa continued, "Alright now, if they let you up, then you have to promise you're done fighting."

I slacked up when I heard his muffled voice saying, "I'm done, I'm done." Pa demanded that we let him up, so Joe and I quickly turned loose and backed away from the man. When he turned around, I realized that he wasn't a man at all. His face was covered in sand, but he looked to be about the same age as Joe and me. His clothes were torn and ripped with holes throughout.

He shouted, "Joe, what are you doing out here with these white men?" Pa and I turned to look at Joe, who seemed to be confused.

"Olomill, is that you?"

After he finished washing the sand from his face in the creek, the stranger quickly walked over to Joe and yelled, "Yeah, it's me! You trying to kill me, Joe?"

Joe sarcastically replied, "Don't reckon you should have ran." Olomill was tall, thin and missing multiple front teeth. I wasn't sure if they had always been missing or if Joe and I had knocked them out. Either way, he was a rough, malnourished-looking character who was just as surprised to see us as we were to see him.

Pa and I were both extremely curious to know how Joe and Olomill were acquainted. Pa spoke up and said, "Olomill, I guess it is. You didn't answer my question about why you are trespassing."

"Well, I grew up here, and it is the only place I know to come back to."

"Come back to?" Pa asked.

"Yes, sir. There has been a lot going on out there in that swamp since the Yankees came through."

"Angus McCrae alluded to something along those lines when we rode over to his place yesterday," Pa said.

Olomill's demeanor quickly changed, and he said, "His men are out there hunting us down like dogs, sir."

Pa looked troubled and said, "Well, Olomill, I hope you aren't in a hurry to get back out there because you are going to help us clean these turkeys and come back home with us."

Olomill looked frightened by what Pa said, but Joe gave him peace of mind when he stepped up. "They are good folk. They are like family now." Pa and I couldn't help but smile when Joe made it clear to Olomill that we did not have bad intentions.

Olomill's mood quickly changed as he apparently trusted Joe, and he began to calm down and relax. Pa offered Olomill a hot meal and a place to stay for the night in exchange for information about what had taken place in the swamp. He gladly agreed, and we began to clean the turkeys in the cool, clear creek water. Pa taught us how to pluck the feathers, remove the innards, and claim the beards, tail fans, and spurs as prizes. Joe and I were both obviously proud of what we had accomplished that morning.

After we removed the tail fans, I couldn't help but feel wasteful as I watched the smaller, beautiful feathers slowly float downstream. If it had been up to me, I would have kept the turkey just like he was for as long as I could, simply so I could admire his beauty. On the other hand, I knew that we were keeping all that we could, and Pa never wasted anything. After we had finished cleaning the turkeys, Pa said, "Alright, let's get on back home so we can put these birds in the smokehouse."

When the four of us emerged from the shaded woods and walked into the bright sunlight, it seemed as if we were leaving one world and entering another. It was back to the real world. Out there in the woods, we normally did not have to deal with struggle, prejudice and hate.

Most of the time, we could breathe deeply and easily as the woods that our Creator provided welcomed us with open arms. Now, suddenly, a heavy feeling hovered above me as I walked behind Olomill and back towards the unknown.

13

Trusting Tildy

The stick that ran from one side of the smoker to the other sagged as Joe and I hung both turkeys on the metal hooks. "That's gonna be a lot of meat," Joe said.

"Those are both big birds, but they may not last us through the night if the work crew gets a taste of it," I joked. After we added hot coals to the smoker and latched the door, Joe and I made our way over to where everyone was working. It was a beautiful and sunny spring day, and everyone around the new homesite seemed to be in high spirits and working together.

Mr. Stubbs was under the shade tree sketching something on a piece of paper, and Pa was talking with Jacob House when Joe and I approached. "Mr. House, what do you have for these two fine young gentlemen to do today?" Pa asked.

"Well, we need someone to carry those fresh-cut boards over to the crew after they have been cut."

"That sounds like a fine job for you two boys. Y'all go get started and remember, the harder you work, the more smoked turkey you get this evening."

Joe and I laughed and made our way over to where two men were cutting the boards. The larger of the two men approached us and asked, "Y'all ever built a house before?"

I quickly replied, "No, sir."

Joe said, "I helped build a few of them cabins over there," as he pointed to the more recently built cabins that served as the slaves' living quarters.

"Good. You ought to catch on quick, then," the man replied.

They told us where to stack the boards and how they wanted them stacked. Our job was to separate the different boards by length, carry them around to the other side of the foundation and stack them neatly. We worked hard all day with nothing but short water breaks to sustain us. By the end of the day, sitting down, kicking my feet up, and eating some of that wild turkey was all that was on my mind. After all, we had been forced to work downwind of the smokehouse and smell it all day.

The temperature began to drop as dusk approached, and Mr. Stubbs called the crew together. We all stopped what we were doing and gathered around to hear what he had to say. "Men, you have done a fine job today, and I'm pleased to announce that we are already ahead of schedule. With that being said, Pastor Harrison has agreed to let each man enjoy his share of smoked turkey for dinner this evening. Eat your fill, gentlemen and get some rest because I intend to accomplish a great deal tomorrow. That is all." Then Stubbs retreated to his favorite spot under the large oak tree.

Pa called us over to one of the cabins after Stubbs was finished and told us to go inside and wake Olomill. Joe said, "You mean to tell me that rascal has been asleep all day while we have been out here working?"

Pa laughed and said, "Well, I figured the boy needed a day of rest after what he had been through. Besides, I plan to fatten him up at dinner. I need him well rested before he tells us about what has been going on across the creek."

The door of the cabin slowly swung open as Joe and I entered. I said, "You wake him up, Joe. I don't know him like you do." Joe agreed and walked up to the side of the bed where Olomill was sleeping. When he shook him, Olomill woke up in a panic as if he did not know where he was.

"Calm down!" Joe said as Olomill quickly jumped out of the bed with a confused look on his face.

"I've been asleep all day?"

"Yeah. Pat and I have been out here working. Don't worry, though, we woke you up just in time to eat."

I urged Olomill to come outside with us, and I could tell that he was still a bit nervous. "Well, you want to eat or not?" Joe asked. Then we led him out the door as Pa called us over to the smokehouse. We carefully transported the turkeys over to where the crew was sitting around a fire and placed them on a table they had recently built. Pa called everyone over, and they formed a circle around us and the food.

After a short moment of silence, Pa called out to God, "Father, despite the circumstances that we find ourselves in, you have still been good to us. I thank you for this crew of fine men that you have sent to help rebuild our home. I thank you for the new friendships and relationships that are being made. We know that you have a plan for each of us, so we pray for your guidance and protection. We ask you to be with our loved ones and give us the strength and wisdom that we need to build this home. We ask that you bless this food to our bodies and our hands to your service. Amen." The group of men all said *amen*, and we began fighting for a spot in line to finally experience the sweet, rewarding taste of a successful hunt.

Pa made sure that Joe and I got one turkey leg each as he loudly declared with a smile on his face, "These two boys killed these birds this morning! Move them to the front of the line!" After we had all gotten our share of the turkey, we gathered around the fire and began to eat. Pa called for Olomill, and after a moment, he slowly came out of the shadows behind everyone. Pa asked him to come sit down beside us as Mr. Stubbs placed a wooden stool beside Pa. Olomill cautiously walked over to the stool, and it was quite obvious that he was nervous about everyone's eyes being fixed on him.

I could hear the men whispering in the background about Olomill's rough appearance when Pa, annoyed by the comments, shouted, "Quiet!" Silence fell over all of us as the men's chatter was reduced to the sound of the wood popping in the hot fire. "Alright, Olomill, tell us what has been going on in the swamp and what you think we can do to help." Olomill looked around at the crew and began to stutter as he struggled to put his words together. We all looked on as he was visibly shaken and becoming emotional.

Joe broke the silence when he stepped forward and said, "Olomill, I told you these were good people. They are only trying to help, and they can't help if you won't let them. Now, I know you don't want to stay out in that swamp."

With tears in his eyes, Olomill looked up from the ground and replied, "There is too much to tell."

Joe, frustrated, took his seat, and Pa said, "Just take your time and start from the beginning."

"They killed my Ma and my two sisters, I reckon. I ain't seen them since we got split up on the first day. The hounds went in behind them, and we heard gunshots later. We ain't seen none of them since. Pa died before we was traded."

"James traded your family to Angus after your father died?" Pa asked.

"I grew up here as a boy working at Bellewood until Master Smith traded us to McCrae. Joe knows. He was there the day it happened. Master Smith was hard, but he wasn't anything like McCrae. He made a sport of removing the flesh from our backs with Pierce's whip. That's why I ran with the rest of them when the Yankees showed up. I'd rather stay out in that swamp than go back and face him or Pierce."

"So, that leads us back to my original question," said Pa. "How did you end up on our property so far from McCrae's plantation?"

"Every time they turn the hounds loose, it pushes us back further into the swamp. It's harder for them to get back to us there. We heard the two shots back there yesterday morning, and they sent me to check it out. We were camped not too far from where y'all ran me down."

"How many more are out there?" Pa asked.

"I'm not sure how many there are, but our group got word that there were more camps like ours. Any slave that did not go with the Yankees or get caught by Pierce and his men is out there in that swamp, sir. They are too scared to come out."

"How many are in your group close to the creek?" Pa asked.

"Ain't but a few of us left, sir. The hounds caught Lindes the other day."

I spoke up and said, "That must have been the day that Pierce and Will McCrae came across the creek on us." It was all starting to add up for me now.

Pa sat there in deep thought and silence for a moment before asking, "If there are only a few of you out there, then where are the rest of McCrae's servants?"

"Most of them went with the Yankees, but a heap of us ran out of the cotton field. We split up the first time the hounds came in after us. Besides the ones that are with us at the creek, I'm not sure who all is left. All I know, sir, is that we are tired of running."

Olomill then bravely stood up and turned his back to the fire. He lifted his ripped shirt to reveal a sight like nothing I had ever seen. The scars ran across his back like streams carved into the landscape. Some wounds were fresh and not yet healed and others were old and scarred over. Olomill winced as the heat from the fire reached the tender skin on his back.

The men in the crew gathered around to get a good look. Stubbs approached Pa, who was in disbelief and said, "Doc, are you prepared to deal with this sort of brutality?"

Pa quickly replied, "It is not yet my fight, but I have a feeling that it soon will be. We will see what tomorrow morning brings, but I plan to ride and talk to the sheriff. Hopefully, Sheriff Morris can send some men out here to put an end to this madness."

Stubbs replied, "I'd be happy to ride with you, Doc. There is no sense in you getting in over your head with people of this sort." Pa nodded his head in silence and turned his attention to Olomill.

"We want to help you, but you're going to have to be brave," Pa said to Olomill. "I know I told you I'd give you a place to stay tonight, but I've had a change of heart. We filled your belly and let you sleep all day, so now I need you to go back to the swamp. Gather everyone in your group who is hungry and willing to come out with you. At daylight, meet us back at the creek where we cleaned the turkeys."

Olomill got quiet and seemed to be thinking about the task at hand. He spoke up and said, "Sir, that's a fine idea, but I'll be surprised if any of them come out of the swamp to meet a white man they don't know. Heck, you had to run me down just to catch me. They are not going to trust you."

"I understand we will have to earn their trust, but if it saves their lives, I'm willing to do that."

Joe quickly said, "I can go with him. They will be more likely to come back with us if I talk to them." Pa quickly shot Joe's idea down and told him that we needed him there with us. I think Pa knew how dangerous it was, and he didn't want to risk Joe getting hurt or even dying in that swamp. Joe seemed to be frustrated with Pa's decision as he slowly walked away from the fire and into the darkness.

Pa and Mr. Stubbs packed a sack full of canteens and leftover turkey meat. Pa sent me to retrieve the lantern that was hanging from the tree beside us, and then he gave it to Olomill. Just before Olomill walked away, Pa called him back and handed him a revolver. After he taught him how to aim and shoot the gun, he sent Olomill off into the darkness. We watched as the light from the lantern moved through the darkness and eventually out of sight.

The next morning, Pa woke Joe and me before the sun came up. We met him outside the cabin, and he told us to grab the two rifles that he had previously given us. Joe and I were both still half asleep, but Pa seemed to be determined. After we got our things together, we mounted our horses and quietly broke camp without waking the others.

I had no idea what the morning would hold, and at that point, I was just following the man I trusted more than anyone, my father. I'd like to say Joe was following him too, but I think he was chasing something bigger. He seemed to be finding out what his purpose was, and he definitely was not backing down from it. After a few minutes of taking our time in the dark and following Pa's lantern, we reached the wood line.

Pa dismounted and motioned for us to do the same as we rode up behind him. "Why are we stopping here? We've still got another hundred yards or so before we reach the path," I said.

"We aren't going to take the path. I don't know what's about to happen, son. I don't know who Olomill will show up with or if he will show up at all. We need to be ready for whatever comes our way. We are going to stay hidden while we watch and listen. Olomill knows the spot, and we will remain hidden until he shows up."

We tied the horses off there and followed behind Pa through the thick woods. We took our time until it started to lighten up some, and then we picked up the pace. Pa stopped about fifty yards short of the creek as the sun began to come up. He began to pace back and forth slowly while he looked for a hiding spot near where we had cleaned the turkeys. Eventually, the three of us sat down at the base of a big oak tree with thick cover between us and that spot.

We could see the spot where Olomill was to meet us through small gaps and holes in the thick brush. Pa said we would hear anybody before we saw them, and I believed him as my eyes struggled to focus. I almost felt like we were hunting, but I didn't have the same peaceful feeling that always accompanied me on a hunt. As the morning went on, the uncertainty grew, and I began to question if they would show up at all.

I was quietly whittling a small stick to pass the time when Pa whispered, "Did y'all hear that?"

"I didn't hear anything. I don't think they are coming, Pa." Then I heard a stick break up ahead and caught movement through the thick brush. Soon after, we could hear water splashing downstream.

"Let's just give it a minute," Pa whispered. My heart rate was rising as a boring situation quickly turned into a serious one.

Moments later, we saw three people quietly making their way across the creek. "I told you they weren't gonna show up. We should have never listened to you," the old man in the back said. Joe and I looked at each other and smirked, realizing that we were completely hidden. Olomill went back and forth, arguing with the older man. The woman had not yet made a noise and seemed to be on edge.

Pa slowly stood up and whispered, "Alright, follow me." When we broke out of the thicket, the three of them almost jumped out of their skin. "Sorry to startle you. We just wanted to make sure that you weren't being followed."

Olomill took a deep breath and said, "Oh, thank God it's you." The older man and the woman looked extremely confused, as if they were waiting for us to speak to them first.

Pa stepped forward and offered to shake hands with the older man as he introduced himself. "Doc Harrison, and what is your name?"

"Washington Eadys, and this here is Matildy, sir," the old man said. Matildy seemed to be shy and nervous.

"Nice to meet you, sir," she softly said. I couldn't blame her for being nervous given the circumstances.

"Where are the others?" Pa asked Olomill.

"Eadys and Tildy were the only two that trusted me enough to come. Everybody has been on edge since we lost Lindes the other day."

"Yeah, I'd imagine so," Pa said. Then he turned and glared at Joe and me until we stepped up and introduced ourselves to Eadys and Tildy.

"How in the world did you end up out here with these white men?" a curious Eadys quietly asked Joe.

"My mama saved Pat's grandma when the Yankees came through. They burned the house and killed her husband. We hid out in the barn with Ms. Elizabeth until Doc and Pat found us. They ain't like them folks that have been after y'all."

Tildy seemed to admire Joe and his courage as she smiled and looked away. I think Eadys was extremely confused about the whole situation. Thankfully, we had the walk back to the new homesite to talk about it. Pa made sure Joe and I gave our horses up to Tildy and Eadys, so we helped them mount up. I am not sure that Eadys would have made the trip back on foot. I was honestly amazed that a man of his age had survived in the swamp to begin with.

He looked to be sixty or seventy years old, and he walked with a limp. The left side of his glasses was shattered, and I wondered why he wore them at all. He sure was curious and also not afraid to speak his mind as he asked question after question. I did my best to answer all of them as I walked behind the horse. It seemed to me the group in the swamp may have chosen Eadys to be the one to decide if our intentions were good or bad.

Tildy, on the other hand, looked to be well taken care of and not as rough as Eadys and Olomill. It also looked as if she had ridden a horse before. My curiosity was buzzing as we approached the homesite. Pa had already made it back and was talking with Mr. Stubbs and House when we tied the horses off.

"Y'all come over here," Pa shouted. Joe, Eadys, Tildy, Olomill and I walked over to where they were talking under the shade tree. "Have a seat," Pa said as he and Stubbs provided Eadys and Tildy a place to sit. The crew had become curious as they stopped working and started listening in on the conversation.

Pa said, "I heard Olomill's side of the story, and now I'd be obliged if you two gave me your personal accounts." Eadys and Tildy looked at each other as if they wanted the other to speak first. "You will not be judged by us or held accountable for anything that you say here today. We only want to help everyone that is in that swamp and bring the people that are doing this to justice."

Eadys proudly said, "I've been with the McCrae family since Angus was a boy. I worked under his father and grew up with him. I've seen him change over the years. I know the hate that he holds in his heart for people like us. I've been on the other end of his whip more times than I can count. Most of the time, he did it for fun.

"When the Yankees come through, I thought about following them out, but I had nowhere to go and nobody to see. I followed the people that I trust into that swamp, and I'd do it all over again if I could. Now, most of them are gone, and if they are alive, we ain't seen them. They got Lindes the other day, and he was the strongest of us all. Now, where does that leave an old man like me?"

"Tildy, how about you?" Pa asked.

"She stayed in the big house! She ain't wanted for nothin'!" Eadys added.

She hesitantly replied, "Well, sir, Eadys is right. I have served Master McCrae in the big house since the day I arrived. He didn't bother me at first until his wife passed away a few years back. Now, if I don't give him what he wants, then he will deliver me over to Pierce and his men. When the Yankees came through the gate, I got scared and ran out the back. I joined everyone else because I couldn't do it anymore. I let that man have his way with me for far too long. My back does not resemble those of Olomill and Eadys, but I have suffered in my own way."

Hearing the personal accounts of Eadys and Tildy seemed to have a profound effect on Pa. I know that it opened my eyes to what we were actually dealing with. Stubbs ordered the men to get back to work, and then he came back to our side. Pa spoke up and said, "I am going to ride to see Sheriff Morris. Stubbs, if you want to join Pat and me, let's go." Stubbs gave his orders to Mr. House, and Pa asked Joe to take care of Eadys and Tildy until we got back.

Afterwards, Pa, Stubbs, and I rode hard toward the jail. When we arrived in Lowndesboro, we saw Sheriff W.C. Morris dismounting his horse outside the jail. Before he could walk through the double doors, Pa shouted, "Sheriff Morris! We need to have a word with you."

The Sheriff replied, "How bout it, Doc? It has been a while. Y'all come on in." So we quickly followed him inside the old jailhouse.

Once inside, we followed Morris into his office and took a seat. He removed his dusty hat and placed his muddy boots across his desk. "What can I do for you boys?"

"Well, it's a long story," Pa said.

"Who do you have here with you today?" Morris asked.

"Well, you know Pat, and this here is Isham Stubbs from Montgomery. He is the contractor who is helping me build our new house. I brought him along so he could serve as an eyewitness."

"An eyewitness to what?" Morris asked.

"To what is going on over on our property line at Bellewood. Angus McCrae is sending his men into that swamp and hunting runaway slaves like they are animals. There is no telling how many they have already killed. I've got three of them sitting with the crew that is building my house at this very moment. They gave me their personal accounts, and it's nothing short of hell out there. They have been pushed back to my property line, and I don't want that mess spilling over onto our property."

Morris, whose demeanor quickly changed, sat quietly for a moment while twiddling his thumbs. "And what exactly do you want me to do about it?"

"I want you to come out there and put a stop to it!"

Stubbs asked, "Sheriff, do you not have any men that you can send to help?"

"Sounds to me like you need an army if you're dealing with Angus McCrae, and that I do not have. In case you haven't noticed, we are running low on soldiers around here."

He continued, "Now, I could take a few men out there, but we would be risking our lives to save a few slaves' necks! What do you want me to tell their wives when they don't come home, Doc? That they were sent to fight for colored folks that they don't even know? Why don't you go home, let this blow over, and allow me to go talk to Angus myself? That sounds good?"

Pa replied, "I should have known not to come up here asking for help."

He then told Stubbs and me to get up as Morris asked, "Now what is that supposed to mean, Doc?"

"It means that it was a waste of time, and that you're probably in his pocket just like everyone else around here. I reckon I'll have to handle it myself!" Pa exclaimed as we walked out through the double doors.

Morris came outside in an attempt to finish the conversation with Pa, but we rode off while he was still talking. The townsfolk were all staring as Morris's words fell on deaf ears. I'm sure that he knew Pa wasn't going to let it rest until someone was brought to justice. Deep down, Pa and I both knew we weren't going to get any help. Stubbs and I struggled to keep up with Pa as we rode back toward the homesite.

Pa was a man on a mission, and I could tell that protecting these people we had just met was becoming his main priority. He always was one to hit everything head-on. Very straightforward, he was often misunderstood, but defending the truth and what was right in God's eyes was always important to him. This situation was no different, as it was obvious that Angus McCrae and his men were committing murder and breaking the law.

Later that evening, Pa showed Tildy the cabin she would be sleeping in, and he also showed Eadys and Olomill where they would be sharing a cabin. It was the cabin next to where Joe and I had been sleeping. "You mean I've got to listen to those two argue back and forth all night?" Joe asked. Joe and I laughed together as we walked off the porch with Pa.

Pa said, "Both of you meet me here at dusk. Make sure the other three are here, too. Now, I've got to get back to work, and our three guests are both of your responsibility. I suggest y'all go down to the sandbar and catch some dinner if you want to eat tonight." Joe's face lit up as I'm sure mine did too when we learned we wouldn't have to work on the house.

We excitedly ran over to Tildy's cabin and discovered that she was already asleep. We decided to let her rest and not trouble her any further. "I reckon she was worn out.", Joe said.

"I would be, too. Come on, let's go get Olomill and Eadys."

When we walked into their cabin, Olomill and Eadys were comfortably lying in their beds, laughing about something. "I thought y'all didn't like each other the way y'all've been arguing since you got here," Joe said.

Eadys replied, "We only argue because we like each other. If I ain't giving you a hard time, then I don't trust you."

Joe smirked and replied, " Whatever you say, old timer."

"Y'all want to go with me and Joe down to the sandbar to catch dinner?" I asked.

There was a moment of awkward silence when Eadys said, "Y'all done gave me a comfortable bed and a roof over my head, and now you want me to walk down to that creek and risk running into Pierce? You must have lost your mind. This old man ain't moving."

"Olomill?" Joe asked.

"I'm with the old man on this one. It ain't worth it, Pat."

Joe joked, "I guess y'all don't want to eat tonight then," and we walked out of the cabin.

Joe and I took the poles we made to catch the Alligator Gar and walked down to the sandbar. The sandbar was much closer than where we caught the Gar and less risky. After we found bait, Joe and I dug our toes into the cool sand and tried our luck. We began to pull catfish out of the calm, deeper water. Every time the line hit the water, we were pulling another fish in. In less than an hour, we had caught a stringer full of fish and enough to feed everyone.

Around dusk, we made our way back up the hill and toward the homesite. The string full of fish was so heavy that Joe and I had to take turns carrying it up the hill. The crew began to shout and cheer as they saw us walking up with the fish. For a short moment there, we felt like heroes.

Pa called us over to the shade tree where he was accompanied by House and Stubbs. "Well, look at y'all! I knew I had hired the right two men for the job!" We smiled and happily accepted the praise. Pa asked House if he and the men could clean the fish before dinner, and then he told Joe and me to gather Tildy, Eadys, and Olomill and meet him at our cabin.

After we woke the three of them, we all met Pa back at our cabin. He was inside, sitting on the bed when we walked in, and he told us all to have a seat. He said, "I've been thinking about this all day since we left talking with the Sheriff. I want to help the three of you, but I also feel obligated to help those who are still in the swamp. The only issue is that we are going to have to send someone back out there to bring them back. Eadys, I know you can't make the trip, and Tildy, I don't want you to have to make the trip, but you are the only one who knows where the camp is. My only choice is to send you and Olomill back to bring the others out before they are injured or killed."

Joe tried to argue with Pa as he realized that Tildy would be put in danger. Surprisingly, instead of choosing fear, Tildy quickly interrupted and said, "I will do it!" It seemed that Olomill was the one who needed convincing, but Pa didn't give him much of a choice after Tildy agreed.

"Olomill, just like last time. You and Tildy go bring them out and meet us in the same place. Assure them that Eadys is here with us, safe and sound. Come outside, fill your bellies, and leave whenever you are ready. We will give you a lantern and a pistol." Pa said. No questions were asked, as what had to be done was clear.

After dinner, Pa and Stubbs brought a lantern, a pistol, and a pack with food and water. Pa then set it all down at Olomill's feet and said, " Best be on your way if you're going to be back at the creek by daylight." Then Olomill agreed, slowly stood up and told Tildy it was time. Tildy took the pack while Olomill carried the lantern and the revolver.

We all wished them well and assured them that we would see them again in the morning. Pa went back over the revolver with them and showed them how to load the extra bullets if need be. Just before they walked away, Joe came over, took Tildy's hand, and said, "Be careful out there tonight."

She nervously smiled and said, "I will, Joe. I plan on seeing you tomorrow."

14

RECONNECTION

Joe, Pa and I quietly settled in under the massive oak tree the next morning as the sun started to come up. We were sitting and waiting in the same place that we had previously met Olomill. The sounds were different in the woods that morning. For some reason, like me, it seemed that even the woods knew a storm was brewing. There was an uneasy feeling in the air, and we had gone from joking around to being serious about the task at hand.

Normally, the owls, crickets and frogs drowned out any distant noises, but that wasn't the case as we listened to the hounds barking deep in the swamp. Pa hadn't said a word since the moment we heard them start up. They seemed to be going the opposite way, but they had covered a great deal of ground already. I could tell Joe was nervous as we all sat there, locked in, moving nothing but our eyes to scan the woods around us. We were all nervous and hoping that Tildy and Olomill would return quickly and safely.

Pa was scolding Joe and me and telling us to sit still when we finally heard something. "Quiet!" Pa said. As I slowly breathed out and everything became quiet, I could clearly hear something running through the woods. It didn't sound like a deer; it was too heavy.

I said, "Whatever it is, it's loud and it's headed right towards us." Instead of waiting like last time, Pa urged us to follow him as he quickly stood and ran down the creek and towards the main crossing.

I followed Joe through the thick brush, and when we emerged, I saw Pa leaned back against the creek bank with his pistol drawn. "Get over here!" he demanded as Joe and I ran toward him. We leaned into the sandy bank, and I pulled my pistol from my side. My blood was pumping when I noticed that Joe was frozen. Pa whispered, "Joe, that pistol ain't gonna pull itself!" He quickly snapped out of his trance, pulled the pistol from his side, and cocked the hammer.

It was hard to hear with our backs to the steep bank. The sound became louder and louder as we prepared ourselves for whatever was coming our way. "I think they are coming around to our right side, Pa," I whispered. It was too late when we realized that we were out of position. We had anticipated them to come to the main crossing, but for some reason, they avoided the open area where we had previously met.

Seconds later, around the corner and out of sight, we heard them hit the water. Pa pushed Joe and me aside as he began to sneak down the edge of the creek and in that direction. The damp sand allowed us to quietly maneuver between the water's edge and the steep bank. I could still hear something breaking through the brush when Pa slowly peered around the turn. His demeanor completely changed as he holstered his pistol and turned back. "Easy boys, it's just Tildy," he said as he let out a sigh of relief.

As Joe and I ran past Pa and toward Tildy, we noticed that she was crying and pointing up toward the thicket. There, we saw Olomill emerging from the thick woods as he was struggling to carry another man. Pa rushed up the sandy bank and relieved Olomill as he fell to the ground exhausted.

I noticed the wounded man's clothes were bloody and ripped to shreds as Pa urged him to gently sit down in the sand. It quickly became obvious that Pa recognized the man who sat before us, moaning in pain.

"What happened?" Pa asked as he frantically searched for the man's wounds.

The man, fighting to catch his breath, said, "I'm looking for my family. Last I saw them, they were at Bellewood, but that's been nearly seven years."

Pa excitedly asked," Levy, is that you?"

"Yes, sir. I'm surprised you recognized me." When Joe heard the conversation, his attention shifted from Tildy to the wounded man. He stood there, frozen and staring. He looked confused as tears began to roll down his face.

"Pop! Is it really you?" Joe nervously shouted. My heart hit my throat as Joe blew past me and toward the man.

"Joe, my boy! I didn't even recognize you. You've grown like a weed!" Joe fell down beside him in the sand, and they passionately embraced each other.

Both crying, they held each other for what seemed like forever until Pa said, "Joe, we need to get him help right now. He is losing a lot of blood. You can talk with him once we get back home. Right now, I need your help."

Joe stood and replied, "Whatever you need, Doc."

"First, I need your shirt. Next, I've seen how fast you are. Now you need to use that God-given gift and run as fast as you can back to the horses. Go get the wagon and bring clean water back with you. Go! Fast!" Joe was shocked as he removed his shirt and saw that it was covered in his father's blood. He handed his shirt to Pa and didn't hesitate before he bolted across the creek and out of sight.

Pa used Joe's shirt to wrap a tourniquet around Levy's leg to slow the bleeding. Levy winced in pain and passed out as the blood flowed down his leg and into the white sand. "Tildy, are you okay?" Pa asked as he noticed her nervously watching.

She replied, "Yes, sir. Anything I can do to help?"

"Just pray that we can get Levy to town and to a doctor."

"Well Pa, aren't you a doctor?" I said.

"I haven't dealt with anything like this in a long time, son. We don't have the supplies we need, and we are going to have to get him to Montgomery."

I saw no way we could make it to Montgomery and past McCrae's men on the main road. Pa asked Tildy and Olomill where the others were. They looked at each other, each expecting the other to answer his question.

Tildy eventually answered, "It was awful, what we saw. When we made it back to the camp, we saw Simon, Mariah and Edmund. They were all hanging from the same tree, and they were already dead. We cut them down and had no choice but to leave them lying there when we found Levy."

Pa began to get emotional and walked down to the water. I imagine he was questioning God about what these people were going through. I was speechless. I had never known such horror in my life. Growing up, I had heard rumors about families that mistreated their servants, but I had never seen it for myself. Pa never allowed us to go over to Grandpa James's place too much because he didn't agree with what was going on. Now, I was seeing it firsthand and found myself right in the middle of it.

Pa, Olomill, Tildy and I sat there in silence while Levy remained unconscious. We were all in shock about what had taken place. Pa prayed and checked Levy's pulse until Joe returned with Stubbs and the wagon. Together, Pa and Stubbs carried Levy across the creek and loaded him into the wagon. Joe said, "Let's go! I've got him!" as we all jumped on the wagon.

Stubbs steered the wagon while Pa attempted to wake Levy to provide him with fresh water. Tildy and I did our best to comfort Joe as he quietly stared at his father. The sorrow that I felt for him was unexplainable. I was glad that he had reunited with Levy, but it scared me that finding him and losing him on the same day was a possibility. I couldn't imagine the thoughts that were going through my best friend's head at that moment in time.

As we were riding up to the homesite, I heard Pa telling Stubbs about the three bodies that were left in the swamp. He said, "Promise me that you will take a few men and retrieve the bodies. Olomill will show you the way. He is bringing the horses back now. If we are not back in two days time, bury the bodies in the pecan grove by the other headstones. They do not deserve to lie out there and rot!"

Stubbs confirmed that he would follow through with it, and when we returned, he helped us prepare the wagon for the trip to town. Pa said, "We have to figure a way to sneak Levy past any prying eyes."

Stubbs quickly replied, "Maybe I can be of service. Follow me." He led us over to where the lumber was stacked and said to his crew, "Come on boys, give us a hand!" He looked at us with a smile on his face and said, "We will hide him in plain sight!"

One by one, we stacked boards on top of each other. We left about eighteen inches of space underneath the stack by running horizontal boards and bracing them up. Afterward, we took sacks and crates to cover up the ends and hide the void. "I believe it will work!" Pa said as he studied Stubb's contraption.

"I know it will work!" Stubbs confidently replied.

Pa got the men to lay Levy out on the grass, and he began to replace the previous tourniquet with a new one. The pain immediately woke Levy as he groaned and attempted to sit up. Stubbs and I held him down until Pa finished. Joe stepped up to calm Levy and tell him that we were going to town to get help. He also told him that he would get to see Lucy and Nan, and that calmed him down until Pa was finished with the tourniquet.

Pa told Levy that he had to remain quiet for the entire trip, no matter what. "That shouldn't be a problem," Joe said as Levy began to pass out again. The men placed blankets in the wagon and slid Levy into the hole, feet first. We covered up the end as everyone wished us luck.

Pa looked at Stubbs before we left and said, "Olomill, Eadys and Tildy are free to come and go as they please, but as long as they are on this property, they are under my protection. I trust you and your men will remember that while we are gone." Stubbs nodded his head in agreement and within a matter of minutes, we were on our way.

"Hopefully, we can make it to the crossroads and out to the main road without any trouble," I thought. A few moments later, my optimism was short-lived when we saw three men on horseback up ahead. "Here we go, boys. Everybody look sharp!" Pa said as we approached the men. I recognized two of the men as being Will McCrae and Pierce. The other man I did not recognize.

"That's Pierce and the other man from the creek. They are probably the ones that shot Pop," Joe said.

"Maybe so, but we aren't in the position to do anything about it right now. Y'all let me do all of the talking," Pa said. I could feel the anxiety consuming me as I thought about what those men were capable of.

Pierce motioned for us to stop as we rode by, but Pa didn't pay him any attention. Pierce and Will McCrae then began yelling for us to stop, and when their requests were not obeyed, they fired their pistols in the air.

Pa brought the wagon to a halt and clutched the pistol at his side. There was no way that we were getting off that easy. The three men rode up and began to circle the wagon.

"Pretty day, ain't it!" Pierce suggested as he came to a stop beside the wagon.

Pa replied, "Yes, it is. Now, if you will let us be on our way, that would be great. We are on a tight schedule."

The three men laughed, and Will said, "Well, right now, it looks like you are on our schedule. Where ya headed today, Doc?"

"Headed to Montgomery to take some of this lumber to my father, and that's about all of the questions I am going to answer. I don't owe you any explanation."

Pierce cut in and said, "I remember these two feisty boys from the creek. I especially remember that one and his daddy." He cut his eyes at Joe. Joe remained quiet, although I could feel the tension building.

Pa said, "Yeah, I've been meaning to talk to you about that, but I tell you what, we are going to head on to town, and I will cut you some slack."

"Cut me some slack, huh?" Tobacco juice ran down Pierce's beard as he spit on the wheel of the wagon and studied its contents. "You ain't seen any McCrae niggers cross that creek, have you?" Pierce asked.

As we slowly pulled away from the men, Pa replied, "We are all children of God, and after the way you treated my family, I don't know that I would tell you if I did."

"Whose side are you on anyway, Doc? By the way, I hung a few of those runaways back by the creek. One of them got away and killed my dog! There's bound to be more close to your place, Doc! Don't make me come looking!" Pa had a look of disgust on his face, but it was quickly replaced with relief as we created distance between us and the men. Pierce was still screaming, but the sound of his voice eventually faded.

It was obvious that the men were trying to get a rise out of Pa, but he did not flinch in the face of temptation, all except for his trigger finger, which was firmly pressed against the trigger guard of his pistol for the entire conversation. Joe had stayed quiet in the face of temptation as well, but from the look in his eyes I gathered that he wanted to rip Pierce's heart from his chest.

"I know those are the men who shot Pop! What are we going to do about it, Doc?" Joe said.

"Well, we passed the first test. Now, we've got to get your Pop fixed up. That is our main priority. If the law won't get involved, I'm not sure what is going to happen. Keep your hands to the plow, Joe. Don't look back and worry about what the enemy is doing around you. Keep your eyes on God, and worry about your family. Think about how excited Lucy and Nan will be to see your Pop."

After we had travelled a few miles, Pa stopped the wagon and walked around to the back. He cautiously removed the sacks and crates behind the lumber and checked on Levy. Afterwards, he quickly ran back to his seat and said, "He is still unconscious, but by the grace of God, he is still breathing." Finally, we had a straight shot towards the river and the city of Montgomery.

"Joe, have you ever been to Montgomery?" Pa asked.

Laughing, Joe replied, "No, sir. I have never been anywhere like that."

"Well, you just stay close to us, and if anybody asks, you tell them that you are with us." Joe didn't seem too worried, but at that moment, he had bigger fish to fry.

"Where are we taking my Pop?"

"To a good friend of my father's, Surgeon Gindrat," Pa replied.

Eventually, we came to the end of the trail and followed the river down toward the city. We started seeing more people, and quite a few of them stared as Pa did his best to smile and wave. It was quite obvious that he was attempting to keep a low profile. When we came to the steep hill just outside the city, we went down and turned toward Grandpa Lewis's house on Church Street. When we got close to the house, Pa told me to jump off and alert Grandpa Lewis. "Tell him to meet us at Charles Gindrat's house," he said.

When the wagon got even with Grandpa's yard, I jumped and rolled in the green grass, and after I got to my feet, I headed toward the front door. Before I could make it to the front steps, I was stopped by Grandpa's gardener. He informed me that my grandparents were at their boarding house down the street. It was in the opposite way that Pa had gone, so I needed to hurry.

Grandpa Lewis and Grandma Jane had an immaculate home on Church Street, but they also owned a boarding house that they rented to Ms. Sarah Pickett. In their older years, they spent a good deal of their time there. I imagine that they enjoyed the company. Their large home on Church Street sat where the Montgomery Post Office was later built.

The first gas lights in Montgomery were used at Grandpa's house. On Church Street, he also hosted the President of the United States, who was our distant cousin, Millard Fillmore. Even though I was younger, I remember Pa taking us to the parade that afternoon. We met the President, and I got to shake his hand and sit with him and Grandpa. They talked about things that I did not yet understand, but I was tickled to be there, and it made me respect my grandfather more than I already did.

I cautiously crossed Church Street and ran as fast as I could down to the boarding house. Grandpa was on the front porch in a rocking chair, talking to an older fellow when I ran up to the front door. "Pat! What in the world are you doing, boy?" Grandpa asked.

Out of breath, I replied, "We need your help, Grandpa! Pa said to meet him at Charles Gindrats!"

As he got up from his chair and headed inside, he mumbled, "What on earth is he doing at Charles Gindrats? Let me tell Jane where we are going. Meet me around the side of the house."

Grandpa met me at his wagon that was situated between the boarding house and the neighbor's house. "Thank goodness, Charles doesn't live far from here. Is someone hurt?"

"Yes, my friend that you met at the cemetery, Joe, his father was hurt badly. The McCrae men shot him in the leg, I believe."

"They shot him? I wasn't aware that he had a father."

"It is a long story, Grandpa," I said.

A few minutes later, we arrived at the surgeon's house, where we saw Pa's wagon awkwardly parked in the yard. He had pulled it through the grass and almost to the front door. "It must be bad," Grandpa mumbled as we came to a halt. I jumped from the wagon and ran to the front door where I was greeted by Gindrat's wife. She had a look of panic on her face as I told her who I was. She welcomed me in before informing me that Pa and Joe were in the living room.

I waited for Grandpa, and we walked into the living room together. Gindrat, whom I had never met, became noticeably aggravated with how many people were in the room. Pa assured him that I wouldn't get in the way as he pointed for me to go and sit beside Joe. They had laid Levy on the living room table, and Gindrat's bloody surgical tools were scattered about. Grandpa walked up to Levy, gently touched his chest, and said, "Lord be with you, Levy. We are praying."

"How bad is it?" Grandpa asked.

"He has lost a lot of blood, but Charles says he will be fine. He has bite wounds on both legs from the hounds, as well as one gunshot wound to the thigh. His hands are also mangled from fighting the hound off. The bullet passed through and missed the bone. He is lucky to be alive." Pa said.

"Who are these godless men?" Grandpa asked.

"Angus McCrae has sent his brute of an overseer to round up each runaway that is seeking refuge in the swamp between his place and Bellewood. They have been hanging, beating, and outright murdering the runaways from what I understand."

Gindrat, a dark-complexioned older Frenchman, stopped stitching Levy's wound and said, "Surely, something is to be done about it!"

"I went and talked to W.C. Morris, and he informed me that he wasn't getting involved with the McCraes. He said he wasn't risking his men's lives to save a few runaway slaves."

Grandpa snarled and said, "Morris and his crew wouldn't be fit for the job anyway. I will go talk to Judge Saffold, and if he won't help us, I will hire someone I trust to do the job. These McCrae men believe they are above the law! Angus has always felt that he was the law around there. This is not a matter of money, but a matter of the heart."

Pa, pacing around the room, said, "I only desire to finish building our home apart from this unnecessary madness. My faith calls me to keep the person that I used to be dead and buried. My old self was crucified with Christ, but when I see the pain and suffering that God's children are going through, I feel called to action. Unfortunately, talks of peace and mercy will not be entertained by these men." Grandpa Lewis was usually quick to respond in a wise manner, but he was silent, and for a moment, he seemed to be lost in his own thoughts.

"How long do you think it will take to get Levy fixed up?" Grandpa asked Gindrat.

"I am close to being finished now, but it will take a while for the ether to wear off." Grandpa then told Joe and me to take the wagon and return to the boarding house to see if mother, Lucy and Nan had returned from shopping. Before I walked out, Pa said, "Take our wagon and bring the girls back, Pat." Then he apologized to Gindrat for leaving the wagon and horses on the well-manicured lawn.

Joe and I quickly approached the boarding house, and we saw the ladies preparing to cross the street up ahead. The first thing I noticed was how fancy the three of them were dressed. Mama was wearing a blue dress, while Lucy and Nan wore matching red dresses. Each one of them had a handful of bags as they crossed the street. "Look at 'em, Joe!" I said. When I looked over at him, he was smiling from ear to ear. Mama, Lucy and Nan couldn't believe what they were seeing as the wagon came to a halt.

"Pat Harrison, what are you doing here?" Mama joked as she dropped her bags and ran up to hug me. Lucy was crying hysterically as she hugged Joe, and his little sister Nan had a firm grip on his leg. Joe and I couldn't stop smiling as we reunited with the ones that meant so much to us. Joe said, "Mr. Doc asked us to bring y'all back down the road to where they are. There is something y'all have to see."

Mama asked where they were, and I replied, "I reckon it is a surprise."

She said, "You know I don't like surprises!"

"You are going to like this one."

When the five of us arrived, Mama said, "Pat, why are we stopping at Charles Gindrat's house?"

I smiled and said, "I guess you will have to wait and see."

When we got to the front steps, Pa opened the door and scooped Mama up. They kissed each other, and Mama said, "I missed you so much!" Then Pa turned his attention to Lucy and Nan. With a smile on his face, he said, "The boys and I rushed a patient who desperately needed a surgeon here. I think you may recognize the man. Before you come in, just know that the ether hasn't completely worn off, but he is fine, and his time spent with Surgeon Gindrat was successful."

Lucy looked confused as she turned to Joe and demanded that he tell her who was in the house. Joe stuck to his guns and stayed silent as Pa led us in through the front door and toward the living room. We walked down the hallway, and when Pa and I entered the living room, I was surprised to see Levy awake and sitting at the living room table. Lucy and Nan were hesitant about coming in, but Joe assured them that everything was fine.

Once Joe had all but forced them into the room, Lucy scanned the room until her eyes met Levy's. At first, she was confused, and it took a minute for her to recognize him. After a moment of silence, Lucy gasped and fell to her knees.

"Who is this man? It can't be! Levy is in Louisiana!" Lucy shouted fiercely as she stared at the floor.

With tears streaming down her face, she slowly looked up as Levy held his arms out and said, "No, Lucy, my girl, I am finally home."

15

LEVY'S STORY

Lucy rushed over and nearly knocked Levy out of his chair when she wrapped her arms around him. "Easy, easy! You're going to rip my stitches out," Levy laughed as he winced in pain. We all thought she was going to squeeze the life out of him, but she finally fell at his feet. Joe walked over and knelt beside his mother, and Levy pulled him in close. There was not a dry eye in the room as everyone watched the family reunite, but for some reason, Nan was keeping her distance.

Levy realized that she was not comfortable and asked Lucy what was wrong with her. Lucy turned and said, "Nan, get over here and see your Pop!" Staring at the floor, Nan shook her head and would not come any closer.

Joe said, "Nan, it's Pop. Come give him a hug." When she wouldn't budge, Lucy picked her up and gently sat her on Levy's knee. She would not look at Levy as he attempted to show her affection.

Levy looked up at Lucy with tears in his eyes, saying, "She doesn't recognize me. It's been seven years, Lucy. She couldn't have been more than a year old when Smith sent me to McCrae's."

Lucy, dumbfounded, asked, "Wait, what do you mean he sent you to McCrae?" Everyone in the room realized then that Lucy did not yet know Levy had only been miles from her for nearly seven years. She began to question Levy when thunder clapped outside of Gindrat's home. We could see the lightning flash outside the window as everyone jumped. Gindrat walked to the doorway and called his two sons downstairs. He told them to go outside and bring the horses around to the barn.

"Another one of those spring showers, I reckon," Lewis said as Gindrat walked back in and closed the door. The clouds moved in quickly as dusk fell on Montgomery. Gindrat's wife brought candles in and spread them throughout the room. As she headed back toward the kitchen, Mama decided that she would join her. It was clear that the situation in her home was making Mrs. Gindrat uncomfortable, and I reckon Mama decided to keep her company.

The thunder continued, and rain started to fall hard outside as everyone in the room listened to what Levy had to say. I know Lucy and Joe were dying to know the truth, but we were on the edge of our seats as well because Levy had not yet been able to tell us his story. It appeared that he was ready to talk when Pa said, "Levy, if us being here makes you uncomfortable and you would like to talk to your family alone, that is perfectly fine with us. We will leave the four of you alone."

Levy quickly responded as he scanned the room and said, "No, everyone here needs to know the truth, and I've got a lot to say.

"Well, the truth is, Master Smith never sold me to a man from Louisiana. I reckon he only told you that so you wouldn't come looking for me. Lucy, Joe, I tried to come back to you. The Good Lord knows that I tried. When Master James sold me to that thieving, murdering devil, he assigned Pierce to look after me. Master James made it clear that McCrae wouldn't be making the purchase unless Pierce was included in the deal. I reckon he wanted to get rid of both of us.

"Pierce watched me like a hawk from the first day we set foot on McCrae's plantation. His evil smirk and dark eyes followed me like my own shadow. After our fight, he made it a priority to make my life miserable, and he did a fine job. I never knew so much hate could live inside of a person until I crossed that man. I quickly learned that McCrae was pulling the strings, but Pierce was pulling the trigger. His heart was dark and cold."

As Levy described Pierce, I began to picture his tobacco-stained teeth and the mischievous grin that hid under his red beard. I don't know that I had ever felt evil in another person, but there was something dark about that man. I could see no good in him. It was as if the racism, hatred, and prejudice in his heart fueled him. I believe if he were forced to stop spewing his hatred onto others, he would have nothing to say. He would have no purpose outside of that.

If not for Levy's voice and the clapping thunder, we could have heard a pin drop in the room. We were all fixed on Levy, and I became so curious that I wrestled with the temptation to rush him through his story. But the more Levy talked, the more I realized that he was an intelligent man. It was obvious that he had been waiting for this moment for a very long time. I believe that time had been appointed by God so that we could get a real grasp on the truth. Levy deserved that time to tell his side of the story.

Levy assured Lucy, "I tried to come to you, but I could never break free. I swear Pierce never slept, and if he had other duties, Angus assigned his son Will to look after me. He is very much like his father, but unlike Angus, Will is young and able-bodied. I tried to talk sense into him, but it cost me more stripes on my back. I believe if I had ever slacked up in the field, they would have killed me.

"Other than being a good worker, they saw me as a dumb nigger with an attitude problem. I reckon they expected me to be happy about being stripped of my family and having to defend the honor of my wife. I could not stand by and watch Pierce rape and abuse my wife! I would not allow it! If I could do it over again, I would do it the same way!"

As I nodded in agreement, Grandpa Lewis came unhinged and yelled, "You mean to tell me this Pierce character was taking advantage of your wife? Was James informed of this before your altercation with the man?" Levy and Lucy were quick to inform us that both James and Elizabeth knew what was going on towards the end.

Lucy said, "I told Miss Elizabeth time and time again, and I believe that my relationship with her was the only reason she made Master James get rid of Pierce. Sadly, my relationship with Miss Elizabeth was not enough to change James's mind about selling Levy. She assured me that everything would be okay."

"Why do you reckon James didn't put a stop to it?" Pa asked.

Grandpa confidently replied, "Men have a way of allowing money to become the number one priority in their lives. I imagine Levy and this Pierce fellow were worth a pretty penny together. In his mind, James thought he was killing two birds with one stone while making a profit at the same time. Unfortunately, he saw Levy as a piece of property and decided that he wasn't worth the hassle of confronting Pierce's actions."

"That's all we were to Smith, and that's all I was to McCrae, a piece of property," Levy said. " As much as I did for that man, he never called the dogs off. It was like being stuck in hell every day. That's why I took advantage of the only opportunity that I had. We had a plan cooked up, but when the Yankees rode up, everything changed. I knew they would be distracted.

"It just so happened that we were planting cotton that morning, and it was all hands on deck. When Pierce and Will rode toward the main house to confront the Yankees, I felt a nudge and a rush of adrenaline. I watched the horses as they made their way down the tree line, and when they turned the corner, I ran faster than I ever had toward the swamp. My family was the only reason that I took the risk. I reckon everyone who was working in that field had their own reasons because, except for a few, they followed me."

Pa interrupted and said, "When the boys and I visited Angus, he mentioned that one of his male negroes had led an escape, and now here you sit, a free man."

Levy replied, "Both Pierce and McCrae knew I was working on an escape plan, but they never expected us to take off in broad daylight. I was afraid we may never get another chance. I feel guilty about those who lost their lives because I decided to run, but I had to get back to my family, and now here they sit, free. Some things, I reckon, are just worth fighting for.

"It took them a little while to find us, but once the hounds got on our trail, they started picking us off one at a time. The ones that were old and slower were the first ones to go, along with most of the women and children. We eventually had to split up and go our own ways. We couldn't afford to stay around the ones that slowed us down. There are only so many places you can hide in that swamp! They hunted us like dogs, and we were forced to hide like cowards! If I ever get my hands on Pierce again, I swear I'm going to kill him!"

Gindrat stood up and said, "Levy, take a deep breath and try to relax. We don't need you getting too worked up."

Lucy said, "Let's take a break and let Levy rest for a minute," but Levy refused to stop, and nobody in the room questioned him.

I admired Levy's tenacity and began thinking that I'd pay a pretty penny to watch Levy get his hands on Pierce. Pierce was a big fellow, but Levy was tall and well-built, and I could see that he had worked his entire life. The man's hands were the size of two of mine put together.

Levy lowered the tone of his voice and tried his best to remain calm as he continued his story. "After they pushed us deep into the swamp, I spent most of my time on a small island that was surrounded by water. The water seemed to slow the hounds down, and when I could hear them coming, I escaped before they got close. The only three things on that island were palmettos, one big tree, and me. I tried to sleep on the ground, but the fire ants were too bad. That first night I climbed up the tree and found a place to temporarily rest.

"The nights were the worst part of being stuck out there. Some nights were so bad that I had thoughts of giving up. Of course, I knew that was not an option. I thought about Lucy, Nan, and Joe to keep me going. After a couple of days, the hunger began to set in. Before that, it was the cottonmouths, mosquitoes, gnats and ticks." Looking around the room, Levy added, "It was hell on earth."

He continued, "We had nothing to start a fire and no weapons to hunt with. We were forced to scavenge, and some of them even ate raw fish and mud bugs. The hunger got so bad that a few of them attempted to make their way out of the swamp in order to surrender. Whether they were successful in their efforts or not, I don't know. Considering Pierce and his posse ran the hounds through there two days later, I'd be willing to bet they gave up our spot in exchange for food and safety.

"As soon as I heard them coming, I broke and ran. I didn't wait for anybody else, and I never slowed down until I ran into a briar thicket. It seemed like the hounds were all around me in every direction. I snuck through the thicket as quietly as possible while the briars pulled at my clothes and ripped my flesh. It took all I had not to lie down and give up.

"When I made it out of the thicket, I stopped and listened for a moment. Everything had finally gone quiet. Just when I thought I had lost the hounds, I heard them pick up my scent again. I knew that they were close, and the only thing that I could do was run. I could barely breathe and my feet were in bad shape, but I knew I couldn't stay there.

"As I ran down through the bottom, I heard a gunshot to my right and felt the pain in my leg. When I stopped behind a tree to look, I saw Mariah, Edmund and Simon being chased by two hounds. Stopping was a mistake because that gave the third blue tick time to catch up with me. He lunged for me and when I tried to stop him, he locked onto my left arm. I continually beat him with my right hand in an attempt to get him to let go. I could feel his teeth sinking deeper and deeper into my skin as we struggled.

"I could hear gunfire and screaming as the hound and I wrestled at the edge of the water. He finally let go of my arm and moved down to my legs. It took everything that I had not to scream, but I didn't want to give up my location. The kicks did not seem to be phasing the hound, and I began to lose hope. As we were fighting for our lives, I picked up a stick and struck the hound on the head.

"He briefly loosened his grip, and I saw my opportunity to grab him around the neck. I grabbed his throat with one hand as he attempted to bite my other hand. His jaws were snapping, and foamy saliva covered his face. Even though he tore my hands up pretty good, I was able to get both hands around his neck. I held on as long and as hard as I could while he fought, and his claws dug into my skin.

"I finally felt the fight leave his body. All of the aggression and energy was no more. I heard talking up ahead, so I kept my head down and quietly hid the dead hound. When I slowly stood in an attempt to see what was going on, I realized that I had been shot in the leg. When I saw all of the blood, I became dizzy and I reckon I passed out.

"When I came to, I could hear the hounds barking and men laughing. I dragged myself to the base of a tree and searched the woods. I saw Pierce and Will with a posse of men torturing Edmund, Mariah and Simon. They were threatening to let the hounds loose as they made jokes and laughed. I was forced to sit and watch as they eventually put ropes around their necks and prepared to hang them.

"I'll never forget the sound of them screaming and crying in the face of certain death. The McCrae men acted as if it were a normal day. They acted as if the situation was nothing out of the ordinary. Perhaps the worst part was having no choice but to sit there and watch my friends die. I was injured and unarmed, and I would have been committing suicide if I had attempted to help them. Still, that made it no easier to watch.

"Pierce made three of the men in the posse dismount, and they put Edmund, Mariah, and Simon on the horses. They threw three ropes over the limbs and put the nooses around their necks. Pierce casually gave the order, and the three men slapped the horses on their backsides. After that, it was over. I refused to watch any further.

"The posse eventually left after confirming they were dead and attempting to call the dog that I had killed. They left my friends hanging there to rot as a warning to the rest of us. After they left, I limped out there hoping to pull them down, but I had no knife and no way to get them down. At some point, I passed out again, and the next people that I saw were Tildy and Olomill."

We were all in shock as Levy let out a sigh of relief and slumped in his chair. Lucy was still upset, and Joe looked to be trying to process everything as we all were. Grandpa Lewis broke the silence, "I've heard all I want to hear! When the rain lets up, I'm going to talk to the Judge!" Pa did not hesitate and confirmed that he would be making the trip with Grandpa as well. He then came over and placed his hand on Levy's shoulder.

"Levy, you are a very resilient man as far as I am concerned. I told Lucy we would all work together, and I'm here to help you however I can."

Levy smirked and said, "Well, I reckon there is one thing you could do for me. Talk to Master James and get me back in his good graces. I want to be where my family is!"

Pa leaned in and quietly said, "Levy, James is dead. The Yankees killed him when they burned Bellewood."

Levy immediately gasped, hung his head, and said, "I'm sorry, I didn't know."

"The estate will eventually belong to my wife, Molly and me."

Levy asked, "If that's the case, then what will happen with my family?"

"Well, my father and I were talking, and we thought it might be a good idea for you to stay at the boarding house for a while with your family. He even said he would find you a good job and that you could stay there until you get on your feet and find a place. He will make sure you are taken care of until you can find a good job, Levy."

"With all due respect, Doc," Levy said, "that's not going to happen. Y'all sit here and act like there aren't more people dying in that swamp! There are more out there, along with the Smith slaves that are yet to come out. We have to go back in and help them!

Gindrat spoke up and said, "Levy, you won't be doing anything for at least two weeks unless you want to end up back here."

"Just do me a favor, Mr. Harrison, will you?" Levy asked.

"What do you have in mind?"

"Allow me to come back to Bellewood, and I will work until I have earned my own piece of ground. I just want to raise my family like any man does."

Pa looked at Grandpa, who shrugged his shoulders, indicating that it wasn't his decision, and reluctantly replied, "Let's get you back to Bellewood, and get you healed up. Then we will talk about the rest later. Your family will have a place to live and food to eat, and you will all remain under my protection until we get all of this sorted out."

Pa shifted his attention to me and said, "Pat, I want you to take everyone to the boarding house while your Grandpa and I go talk to the judge. Find Levy a comfortable room, and we will be back when we are finished." I nodded in agreement as Pa and Grandpa told Mama where they were going and walked out the front door. The quick spring shower had blown by almost like the intense moment that we had all shared inside Gindrat's home. It was dark and ugly for a moment, but now the sun was trying to peek through.

The next morning, we all met on the front porch of the boarding house. Grandpa was sad to inform us that, despite his connections with Judge Saffold, we would not be getting any immediate assistance. The judge said that he would pass the word along to the chief of police and recommend that they send a group of men to help. He hinted that it may take a while and that it wouldn't be wise to retaliate. Pa was none too pleased to hear that we would be on our own.

We stayed in Montgomery for a couple more days so that Levy could heal enough to make the trip home. He mainly slept while he was there. I guess he finally had what he was looking for and needed to rest up from what it took to get it. Mama, Elizabeth, Jane and I did some shopping for Tildy, Eadys and Olomill. We all appreciated being able to spend time together before we split back up. As badly as I wanted Mama to make the trip back, I knew it wasn't a good place for the women to be.

On the fourth day, we made the trip back to Bellewood. It was Pa, Joe, Levy, and me. We were loaded down with supplies and eager to return. Pa took us the long way around so that we could avoid Pierce and his men. We had traveled a good distance when I noticed that there were three horsemen who had been following us since we left town. They had been keeping their distance, and when I asked Pa who they were, he said, "Your Grandpa hired a few guns to help us with what is to come. Boys, whether we like it or not, I feel a fight coming."

16

THE RETURN

"We should wait for the law! It has only been two weeks, Levy!" Pa said as he quickly followed Levy away from our newly erected home.

"Only two weeks? That is two more weeks that they have had to survive out there with no food or water! They will die if we don't help, Doc!" Levy exclaimed. Pa had been wrestling with the fact that Levy would soon heal up and wish to save everyone in the swamp. I know Pa had a desire to save everyone as well, but he did not desire to dig up an old version of himself that would cause him to be disobedient to God.

Levy said, "Doc, out of respect for you and what you have done for me and my family, I have waited this long. Joe, I and whoever is capable of joining will be going back and saving as many as we can. I'm not fully healed, but I am ready to do what needs to be done. I have friends out there, and I can not turn a blind eye!"

Pa replied, "I completely understand your decision, and I will be praying for your safety."

Joe and I had been trailing Pa and Levy since they walked off the front porch. I spoke up and said, "If Joe is going, then I want to go, too." Pa stopped and gave me a look that I had only seen once or twice in my entire life, and I wasn't man enough to question him.

"You'll be staying here, Pat. Lord willing, the law will finally show up before this gets any worse. My job is to protect you, son." I feared that something bad was going to happen, and I wouldn't be there to help my best friend.

"Well, if I can't talk you out of going, Levy, then I don't reckon I can let y'all go out there without any help." He then summoned the three young men whom Grandpa had hired in Montgomery and asked them to accompany Levy. They gladly agreed, and it was probably because they had done nothing over the last two weeks but help finish the house. I imagine they were anxious and itching for a little action.

We had gotten to know the three brothers from Plantersville quite well over the last couple of weeks. Randall, the oldest brother, was a burly, intimidating character and a man of few words. It was easy to see that his two younger brothers, Isaac and Luke, looked up to him. Isaac and Luke, who were in much better shape than their older brother, favored each other so much that you could mistake them for twins. Randall seemed to be calm and calculating, while it was obvious that Isaac and Luke were the loose cannons. Isaac and Luke would often step out of line, but Randall always held them accountable.

While Levy, Joe, and the rest of the group prepared to depart, Pa went back inside and came out with what looked like a brand new rifle. The gun looked like it had never been fired, and she was a beauty. The Henry lever-action .44 had gold plating on the side and a beautiful walnut stock. Pa walked up to Levy and said, "This gun belongs to my father. He ordered it from New Haven, Connecticut. He sent it back with me and said he hoped we wouldn't need it. It looks like the time has come, and if you promise to take care of it, I'd be glad for you to carry it with you today."

"I'd be honored to use it, Doc," Levy said as he gladly took the rifle while admiring its beauty. We could all see that in his heart, Pa wanted to go with Levy, but his convictions were too strong. At that time, he couldn't afford to become reckless because it would have cost us all. We needed him and his strong, unwavering leadership. Without it, we would have all gone down in a blaze of glory within a day's time.

Honestly, when it came to manpower, we were under the impression that we would be heavily outmatched. We had no clue what we were up against, and quite frankly, it didn't matter. Levy and Pa had no issue with anyone but Pierce and Angus and Will McCrae. They agreed that cutting the head off the snake could end this ordeal once and for all, although Pa and Levy's ideas of justice were two different things.

The crew that went out that first afternoon consisted of Levy, Joe, Olomill, Tildy, and the three brothers that Grandpa hired. They were well supplied, armed and ready to venture into the unknown. We all tried to talk Tildy out of going with the crew, but she assured Levy that she could be of assistance. I believe she refused to stay home because she was afraid of losing her newly found relationship with Joe. Randall and his brothers surely did not like the fact that Tildy would be tagging along, and they made that known.

Before they mounted their horses, I made my way over to Joe. Oddly, he had been very quiet since Levy announced that they would be heading into the swamp. "I wish I were going out there with you, Joe. It's not because I don't want to. Pa isn't going to let me go out there because he is afraid that something bad will happen. He just lost Mason, and I don't think he is ready to lose anybody else. Be careful out there, and if things go bad, shoot straight."

Joe shook my hand and said, "I know if it was up to you, you would be right there with us. I reckon you can do your part here too, by praying to that God y'all talk to so much. Ask him to take these butterflies out of my stomach." We both laughed, and I assured him that we would be praying for a safe trip and a safe return. They did not have far to travel, but once they crossed the creek, all bets were off.

Before they left, Pa said a prayer over everyone. He asked God to protect them and allow them to return safely and successfully. Whether they personally knew Jesus or not, I think they all felt better after Pa's passionate prayer. As they rode off, all I could think about was how badly I wanted to go with them. I was there with my father, and my mother was in town, but for some reason, I felt like my family was riding away from me.

Frustrated, I began to quickly walk back toward the house. As I walked away, Pa said, "Pat, I know you are angry, but one day you will understand." I knew that I would never understand letting my friend ride into danger without me being there to help him."

After the crew left, I went inside and lay down. I thought about what Pa may have meant when he said that, but I couldn't see past my own desires. I had become bitter with my father, and I was blinded to the fact that he was just trying to protect me.

Later that night, I was awakened by the sound of a gunshot. When I walked out on the porch, I could hear nothing other than the crickets and frogs. I wondered if they had found anyone yet, and if anyone had been harmed. I also started to wonder if I had actually heard the shot in a dream. The lightning bugs floated by in the darkness, and I asked God how something could be so beautiful while something so ugly was taking place. What little rest I got that night was on the porch while I listened and waited for their return.

The next morning, Pa shook me and woke me up. "Why did you sleep out here, son?"

"Pa, you know why. Are they back yet?" For the next couple of hours, I kept my mind occupied by whitewashing the new wooden fence that surrounded our home. Stubbs, House and the crew had done a fine job and built a beautiful home for our family. The only things that we lacked were a little paint and the women to make it a home. But understandably, Pa still wasn't ready for the girls to come home.

I had almost finished the front stretch of fence when I heard Pa call out, "Pat! You'd better come look at this!" When I ran around the corner of the house, I could not believe what I was seeing. Levy and Joe were leading a large group of people toward the house. I wanted to run as fast as possible to the group, but I held back my excitement the best I could. I felt so relieved when I saw Joe riding proudly behind his father.

When they got close to the house, I couldn't contain myself any longer. I ran out to greet Joe, but I was also greeted by a large group of previous Smith slaves. I recognized some of them, while I was not familiar with some of the others. There were women and young children who could barely hold themselves up. I wondered how they had survived out there for that amount of time. They seemed to be worn down and hanging on by a thread as the last few made their way over toward us.

Levy brought up a white man that I had never seen with a rope tied around his hands. "This one was out there on patrol by himself," Levy said.

Randall added, "Yep, we made quick work of him. All it took was a warning shot to get him to quit! Looks like McCrae is hiring cowards and not soldiers to do his dirty work." Pa seemed to be in shock and hadn't said a word since they had arrived. He quickly walked past us toward the large group of runaways where an old man was lying on the ground.

Pa walked up and kneeled down beside him. The woman at his side spoke up and said, "He is dying, Doc. They shot him two days ago, and he has been hanging on ever since."

"Hello, Milly," Pa said. "I'm sorry to see you under these circumstances, but you are safe now. Bob, my old friend, what have they done to you?"

Milly quickly replied, "Being his usual stubborn self, he wouldn't listen to me and went out there and got shot!"

Pa examined the gunshot wounds on Bob's chest and stomach. He told Milly that they were infected and that the wounds were likely fatal. I believe she had already accepted the fact that he wasn't going to make it. Her only reply was, "Well, ain't you a preacher down there at the church?"

"Well, yes ma'am, I am."

"Can't you pray for him or something?"

"I have an even better idea. Y'all help me get him on the wagon," Pa said.

Isaac and Luke stepped up and carefully placed Bob on the back of the wagon. Pa looked around and loudly said, "If you are able to walk, follow me down to the creek."

Everyone looked around like he was a crazy man, and Levy said, "Doc, the only reason they came back was because I told them James had passed away. I don't think they want to go anywhere near that creek for a while."

Pa replied, "We will only go down the hill and stay close! I am trying to save this man's life." He then looked down at Bob and asked, "Bob, do you know Jesus?"

Bob weakly replied, "No, sir, I've heard about him, though."

"It doesn't look like you have much time left, Bob. Would you like to hear the gospel of Jesus Christ?"

"Yes, sir, I reckon so. I ain't got much to lose."

After Bob's quick decision, I steered the wagon down toward the creek as Milly and Pa rode beside Bob on the back. Pa proudly shared the gospel with Bob and told him how much Jesus loved him. A large crowd followed as we were all interested to see what was going to happen. Isaac, Luke, Joe, and I slowly carried Bob down to the edge of the creek. Pa said, "Further, carry him into the deeper water."

When we were waist-deep in the cool water, Pa told us to stop as he waded across the creek toward us. "Praise God!" he said as he approached us. Everyone standing on the banks, myself included, wondered how Pa could be full of joy at a time like this. This man was dying and probably wouldn't make it through the night.

"Alright, boys, I've got him," Pa said as we let go of Bob, and he floated into the hands of my father. Pa loudly said, "It may feel like there is no reason to celebrate today, but I am here to tell you that there is. This man has decided to accept Christ and make it public by being baptized in the waters of this creek. This is good news! His old life and sin will be washed away downstream forever. He will become a new creation in Christ, and he will spend eternity in heaven with God. Though this life is passing away for him, he will have eternal life in heaven through Jesus Christ."

Pa always talked about how Jesus taught with authority, and in that moment I saw why it was so effective. Everyone but Pa thought it was a time of mourning. In his eyes, he was doing what Jesus told us to do. He was sure of it, he was confident, and he had faith that even though Bob was dying, he was really being born again. That sort of behavior commanded our attention and respect.

As the blood from Bob's wounds washed downstream, Pa asked him, "Bob, do you accept Jesus Christ as your personal Lord and Savior?" When Bob nodded his head, Pa said, "Upon your profession of faith, I now baptize you in the name of the Father, the Son, and the Holy Spirit." Then he slowly dipped Bob's body underwater and quickly lifted him back up. A huge smile came across Bob's face as he wiped the water from his eyes. I was scared to look around because I didn't want anybody to see the tears in my eyes. Then the brothers, Joe and I, carried him back to the sandy bank while Pa clapped and praised God. Everyone else seemed to be slightly confused, and when Pa asked if anyone else wanted to learn about Jesus, no one stepped forward.

When we all made it back up the hill, I made it a point to talk to Joe and ask him how everything went. He was occupied with Tildy and another young woman whom I recognized but couldn't place in my mind. As I walked up, Tildy said, "Pat, this is my sister, Fannie Mae."

Joe spoke up and asked, "Yeah, Pat, you remember her from Angus McCrae's place, right?" That's where I knew her from! I was surprised that I had forgotten her name because I surely hadn't forgotten her face. She was pretty, just like her sister Tildy.

"How in the world did you find her?" I asked Tildy and Joe.

Before they could answer, Fannie Mae said, "After everyone else left, Angus started losing his mind, and one night when he was asleep I ran. I eventually ran into everyone you see here. They took me in and let me hide out with them. I am grateful for them. I would not be alive if Milly, Minerva, and Hannah hadn't helped me."

With a smile on her face, Tildy jabbed Joe and said, "I told you there was a reason I needed to go!" Joe laughed and then accepted my invitation over to the table under one of the large oak trees. I had to know what I missed. "What was it like? What happened out there?" I asked.

"You didn't miss too much. Randall could have killed the man who works for McCrae, but Pop told him to fire a warning shot instead. We saw his lantern through the woods, and the three brothers snuck up close to him. When they surprised him and fired a warning shot, he got off that horse real quick!" We both laughed, and Joe added, "On the way back, we came across their camp. They had been hiding out under everyone's noses, not too far past where we killed the turkeys. A few of them ran when they saw the brothers, but most of them recognized us. Milly said they only had the one incident with McCrae's men when old Bob got shot."

"Dang, so it was that easy, huh?" I asked.

"I wouldn't say it was easy, but it went smoother than I thought it would. Deep down, I was hoping we would run into Pierce, but I would have had to beat Pop to him."

I replied, "Well, I don't imagine it will take long when that man y'all captured doesn't show back up."

"Yeah, I think that was Pop's plan. He wants to draw him out and get him in a place where we have the advantage. We are going back tonight after we catch up on some rest. Pop wants to try to find the rest of them. He ain't taking no for an answer."

I sat there in silence as the intruding thoughts took over my mind. I knew what Pa had said was right, and I knew what I felt in my heart was right. I began to think of a plan to sneak away and ride with Joe to the swamp.

"I know what you're thinking, and Doc is going to skin you alive if you are serious," Joe said. I knew Joe was right, but I was willing to trade a butt whipping to help my friends. I just wished Pa would lighten up, but the chances of that happening were slim to none.

During our conversation, I noticed all of the previous slaves from Bellewood were moving back into the cabins in which they previously lived. Their spirits seemed to be lifting as they realized we had no ulterior motives or bad intentions. Pa just wanted to provide them with food and protection, and most importantly, share the gospel with them. I think that he wanted to prove to them that he didn't view them as property, but as equals and children of God.

Eadys was angry and mumbling under his breath as he limped past Joe and me. Joe and I had just watched the old man get politely kicked out of Milly's cabin. I don't reckon we would have laughed so hard if Eadys weren't so ornery all of the time. He was a loner and seemed to watch everyone at all times. He was as old and wise as he was ornery and bitter.

Joe and I carried on our conversation as Eadys stumbled over toward the McCrae prisoner. The man had been tied up there all day, and for the most part, everyone left him alone. He hadn't said a word other than asking for water. I had a feeling that he wasn't going to willingly give Pa the information that he wanted. The young man had a foreign accent, and it was obvious that he wasn't from around here.

Moments later, I heard a whip crack and Pa yelling, "Eadys, don't do it!" at the top of his lungs. When I turned back, I saw Eadys with the whip in his hand standing over the defenseless prisoner. He began going to town on the young man while he rolled around in the dirt in an attempt to avoid the whip. Eadys laughed and yelled, "How do you like that, boy?" Pa broke and ran to take the whip from Eadys, but not before he left a mark. The man rolled and whimpered as Eadys finally dropped the whip at Pa's feet and walked away.

I was dumbfounded at the boldness of the old man. He was confident and unbothered by what he had done as he started to make his way toward the only cabin that wasn't occupied. Pa yelled at him, "Eadys! Stop! That is not how we handle things around here."

Eadys came to a stop and looked toward the ground then turned and said, "Oh, is that right, Doc? Well, explain this then." The old man pulled up his shirt and turned to reveal the most gruesome thing I had ever seen. Olomill's back was nothing in comparison to the mangled back of Eadys.

Pa could not respond. He stood there quietly, while Eadys dropped his shirt and went on his way. There was nothing he could say, and we both knew that. After the crowd cleared, Pa went over and checked on the prisoner and sat him up. He brought him some water and made it known that he was to be left alone.

All day, we sat under the shade trees and listened as Levy devised a plan for their second trip to the swamp. Milly, Hannah, and two of the men, Obadiah and Tobias, drew a map out for Levy to study. The large group had somehow remained hidden, avoiding most of the action. It seemed that they had learned the land pretty well based on the map that they had drawn. Levy studied the map and talked about going much further down the creek on our property instead of covering so much ground on McCrae's property. He claimed to know the area where the remainder of the McCrae runaways would be hiding.

Joe was correct that the place where they had hidden wasn't very far past where we had turkey hunted. Levy planned to leave the horses and some of the supplies at the old camp where Fannie Mae and the others were previously hiding. This would make it possible to sneak in behind the McCrae runaways and possibly save them all without a fight. I knew exactly where he was talking about, and the intruding thoughts of defying my father's commands consumed me.

I had decided that the risk was worth the reward, but I still needed to come up with a plan. Joe and I locked eyes, and he knew that I was scheming. We didn't have to say a word to each other. He knew that I wanted to be out there with them, and I knew that he understood why. "You'd better go ask Doc one last time," Joe said.

"It's a lost cause, but I will try. I'm going to have to wait until dark to leave, so I need you to hold Levy up as long as possible. Make sure you get my horse ready and have him waiting for me in the barn. I'll meet you at the old campsite on the map."

"I'll do my best, but I can't make any promises."

I went and found Pa just before dusk and confronted him one last time. "Pa, I really think I need to be out there with Joe and Levy tonight. They may need my help."

Pa quickly replied, "Pat, I've already told you. Don't ask me again." I had a lump in my throat as I fought to hold back the tears of anger. I stormed inside and slammed the door behind me while Pa was still trying to talk.

I went down the hall into my room and lay down in bed. I thought, "This is exactly what I did last night, and I didn't see Pa until the next morning. Maybe I could just let him think that I was angry and pouting in my room until it was time for bed." I then gathered everything that I could find in my room to stuff under the blankets and make it look like I was lying in bed. If Pa came into my room, it was over anyway. My plan was simple. I would wait until after the crew left and Pa had dropped his guard. Then I would make my move and show Joe that I was willing to risk receiving the worst beating of my life to be there for him.

17

LEVY'S REVENGE

I'd be lying if I said that I wasn't nervous and maybe even a little scared. The swamp was dangerous, no doubt, but I was more worried about the wrath of my father when he found out that I had disobeyed him. I had always respected him so much that I never even considered blatantly disobeying him. This would be the first time that I went out of my way to lie to my father and go against his wishes.

I watched out the window as Levy, Joe, and the rest of the crew made their way toward the back of the property and the old campsite. Pa saw them off and then disappeared around the side of the house. My heart was beating inside my chest as I began to question whether I was serious about sneaking away or not. The more I wrestled with it, the more I realized that I needed to be there for my friend. So I decided to wait a few minutes, make sure Pa wasn't coming inside, and then sneak out.

It was risky not knowing where he was, but I knew that I had to rush to the old campsite before Levy and the crew left me behind. It wasn't quite dark, but it wouldn't be long before Pa would call it a day. He would likely assume that I was frustrated with him and keep his distance until I was over it. If I were wrong, I would be toting a butt whipping like never before.

When I made it to the door, I decided it would be wise to carry my rifle up against my leg and not wave it around for everyone to see. I slowly walked off the back porch, looking over my shoulder for Pa until I reached the barn. I peeked through the cracks in the old boards and didn't see Pa anywhere. Everything was quiet, and I knew that this was my opportunity.

As I untied my horse, I thought about the consequences of the decision that I was making. I then saw where Joe had filled my side pouch with .44 cartridges, and that was a quick reminder for me that I was doing the right thing for the right people. I couldn't afford to carry a lantern, so it would be a race against the dark. I had already planned to cut it loose and not look back anyway.

I eased the black mare down through the other horses until I reached the far end of the barn. One last time, I peeked around the corner and made sure that Pa wouldn't see me. After a few moments of praying and fighting the urge to change my mind, I mounted my horse and dug my heels into her side. We shot out of the barn like we were fired from a cannon. The black mare pulled with everything that she had as we skirted the pasture and followed the tree line down. I never looked back until we were out of sight.

I was confident that Pa had not seen me, but I was worried that someone else had. All I needed was time, and once my adrenaline started pumping, I knew that I was ready to face the consequences of my actions like a man. I thought that I knew what was ahead, what was waiting for me in that swamp. My vision was clear, and I was sure of what I had to do as I left the shame and guilt of betraying my father behind me.

Riding hard, I passed the logging trail where I usually accessed the creek and followed the field edge around the bend. The fields to my right were separated by small fingers of woods and streams that were fed by the creek. Based on what I had seen on the map, I followed the fields all the way back until I ran into the property line. I dismounted there and led my horse into the dark woods. I slowly made my way down to the creek, searching for tracks along the water's edge.

I became nervous when I could not find any tracks between there and the property line. I quickly backtracked until I found where the crew had crossed. They too had dismounted and walked in by foot. I was running out of time as I had not taken into consideration the woods being darker than the fields. I wasn't sure how far I had to travel, but I followed the tracks across the creek and into enemy territory.

The crew's trail weaved through the beaver lakes and low spots in the swamp. The old cypress trees towered over me, and I began to feel like I was going in circles. Everything around me looked the same as I searched for landmarks. I quickly learned to keep my head down and stay focused on the tracks. Eventually, I ran into water, and my only choice was to cross. There was no one in sight as I led my horse into the dark, murky water.

I was sure that I was lost, but I kept thinking back on the simplicity of the map. I knew where I was going; I had just never been there before. I no longer had the fresh tracks to serve as a guide, and that was intimidating. The hidden cypress knees that were beneath the surface tripped me up as I nervously pushed forward. Just before I began to panic and believe that I was lost, I heard voices ahead of me.

I immediately leaned back against a cypress tree and did my best not to move. The ripples made their way across the top of the water and in the direction of the voices. I began to wonder if I had mistakenly stumbled up on McCrae's men. Then I remembered what Levy had told the crew earlier in the day. He said, "If you get lost or separated from the group, do your best to sound like a hoot owl. That way, we know who you are in the dark."

Luckily, thanks to my father, I was very well rehearsed in mimicking the sound of an owl. When I was a young boy, we would sit outside at dusk and talk back and forth with the owls that lived around our home. I never knew it would come in handy down the road, but a lot of things that Pa taught me were beneficial later in life. As I studied the dark shapes moving around in front of me, I let out my best rendition of a Great Horned Owl.

The voices in front of me went silent, and I was quickly met with a response from that direction. I let out a sigh of relief and coaxed my horse through the cypress knees. The voices became more clear as I could barely see the men coming out into the water to greet me. "Pat! I never thought you would do it!" Joe said as he waded through the water. Then I felt a large hand grab me on the shoulder, and I turned to come face to face with Levy.

"Does Doc know that you are out here?"

"Well, no, sir. That wasn't going to stop me, though."

He was visibly frustrated, "I don't reckon you are going to listen to me if I tell you to go back, but I will be sure to let Doc know that you and Joe had this planned. It's too late to take you back now." He then took my horse from me and told me to follow him. When he passed Joe, he poked him in the chest and said, "I know you played a part in this."

The truth is, Joe and I were both willing to do what we had to do despite the punishment. Sitting back and allowing these people to die was no longer an option. We smirked at each other as Levy led my horse onto dry land. Joe put his arm around me as we waded through the water and said, "I really didn't think you would do it."

I laughed, "There for a while, I didn't think that I would do it either."

Once we were on dry land, I saw Randall, Isaac, Luke, Olomill, Obadiah and Tobias. In all, there were nine of us. Randall was cleaning his rifle while Isaac and Luke sharpened their knives. Obadiah and Tobias were bickering back and forth as they often did. The Smith runaways had hidden on a small island a lot like the island Levy had hidden on. The horses were tied off, and we used what little light we had left to make sure everyone had a sufficient amount of ammunition.

My heart skipped a beat when I heard Levy say, "It's time. Fall in line, and everybody stay close." I watched as he proudly pulled Grandpa's rifle from the scabbard on his horse. The gold plating shone in the low light as he led us off the island and through the knee-deep water.

Randall said, "Y'all promise me one thing. If for some reason, I don't make it, bury me in that pretty pecan grove up there. If Luke and Isaac don't make it, I don't care what you do with them." Isaac splashed water on his brother as they laughed through the tension.

Levy stopped and said, "We are all going to make it out of here! We are going to walk until we find them. Keep your voices down and don't stop unless the man in front of you stops." We were no longer relying on the map, but on Levy's knowledge of the woods. He seemed confident, and that kept our spirits high as we reached the other side and followed him onto dry land.

He led us to a small ditch, and we followed it down until we hit water again. We were moving so slowly that it was hard to tell how much ground we were covering. Olomill whispered, "I can't see anything."

"Grab hold of my shirt and walk!" Obadiah whispered. Levy remained silent as he frequently stopped to listen to our surroundings. We could hear the slightest of noises. It was obvious that we were the only humans ignorant or brave enough to be knee deep in that water without a light to guide our way.

Levy finally stopped after what seemed like an hour of creeping. We all sat down and poured the water from our boots as Levy assured us there was nothing but dry land between us and the runaways. "We aren't far!" he said as we regrouped and waited for the next move. Then Levy slowly stood from where he was kneeling and hooted like an owl. Five or ten seconds later, we heard a reply in the distance.

Levy became excited and urged us to follow him, but Randall was uneasy. "Y'all hold up a minute! That could very well be a real owl replying to you, Levy."

I couldn't say that I did not agree with Randall, but Levy said, "Listen up!" and then he perfectly whistled like a whippoorwill. I had never heard anything like it. Sure enough, a few seconds later, someone whistled back.

"Okay, okay, let's go," Randall said, as we fell in line behind Levy.

Before we went any further, Levy stopped and asked me and the brothers to stay behind. He said, "No hard feelings, but we don't need to march in there with four armed white men. When you hear me whistle, come on." We agreed to stay behind as Levy finally lit his lantern and Joe, Olomill, Obadiah and Tobias walked in to meet the runaways.

Isaac and Luke argued back and forth as we stood there and fought the swarms of mosquitoes. "Quiet!" Randall said as we listened for Levy's whistle. For the next thirty minutes, the whistle never came. I was growing impatient with the argumentative brothers when we finally heard the whistle come in the distance. We quickly followed each other toward the sound until we came to where the runaways were hiding.

Levy was in the process of convincing everyone that we were only there to help protect them and get them out of the swamp. When we walked up, there looked to be at least a dozen runaways consisting of men, women and children. Their eyes were all locked on us, and I imagine it's because we all looked like the men who had made their lives a living hell. I felt nothing but sorrow for them as I realized what kind of shape they were in. They were skin and bones, and their clothes had been reduced to rags.

Levy was mainly talking to one man who seemed to be the group's leader. He told him that they were to follow us out of the swamp as quietly as possible. The large man assured Levy, "If what you say is true, we are ready to follow you."

"You don't trust me? After all we have been through together? Do you think that I would lead you astray, George?"

"No," the man replied. "I trust you. It is just that we have made it out here this long, and I don't want to run into the wrong end of a rifle."

"We'd better get going," Randall said as Levy and George continued to talk.

Levy told the man, "If things go south, you get everybody across the creek on Harrison property. Don't wait on us! We will hold them off until you get them to safety." The man nervously agreed and rounded the group up. He told them to stay close and stay quiet. He placed one child on his shoulders and ordered the other men to do the same.

As we started our journey back toward the horses, Randall asked Levy, "Are you gonna snuff that light out?"

Levy shrugged, "There is no way that they make it back in the dark."

"They won't make it back if they are dead, either," Luke added.

Randall said, "Yeah, let's take it slow in the dark like we did on our way in here. There is no need to draw attention to ourselves."

Levy agreed to go out just like we came in, and as we entered back into the water, the world became dark again. As the light went out, I heard the women gasp behind us. If they didn't have enough reason to be afraid, they did now. I could hear the children in back whining and someone whispering, "Y'all can't be making all of that noise now." Our eyes were useless; we depended only on our ears and the people in front of us.

Levy and the brothers led the party, followed by Joe, me, and then everyone else. For some reason, I wasn't as nervous as I was when we went into the swamp. On the way in, I was worried about getting lost. Levy proved to us that he knew the ground, and that was enough for me. He had gotten us in safely and cleanly. I truly believed that he could do the same on the way out.

Every time one of the children began to cry or make unwanted noises, Levy would stop, wait, and listen. For the most part, we moved through the swamp quietly, but when the silence was broken, it sent a chill down my spine. I did my best to stay positive and think about the outcome that we wanted. I thought, "Well, if we all make it back safely, maybe I can celebrate after Pa finishes ripping me a new one."

Levy whispered, "Almost there," and we all passed the word down the line. I heard when Levy's feet hit dry ground. He cautioned everyone to wait for a moment while he walked out a little further. After he had listened for a moment, he quietly whistled for us to move forward and out of the water.

We all made it out, but before Levy could lead us to the ditch we had followed in, I saw a small light become visible in the distance. "Levy, do you see that?" Then the light grew brighter and brighter, and more lights around it began to light up the darkness.

The unmistakable cracking sound of a rifle pierced through the silence, and all hell broke loose. "Get them out of here!" Levy yelled as the woods lit up with gunfire. I could hear the bullets zipping through the air as I retreated to the base of a cypress tree.

"Joe, over here!" I yelled as he crawled toward me in the darkness.

"Where is Pop?" Joe asked as he attempted to stand. I pulled him back down and told him that we had to wait for the gunfire to stop.

I clutched that rifle like I never had before as we dug in at the base of the tree. After a few minutes, the shots stopped, and I heard the men yelling back and forth. I could hear the large group tearing through the swamp behind us. "At least they will make it out of here," I thought. The sound of an owl broke the silence, and Joe and I immediately responded. Then, all around us, Joe and I heard several responses.

"Well, there are at least eight of us still alive!" I said to Joe.

"We've got to find Pop!" he insisted.

Joe and I decided to stay low and crawl toward the first owl hoot that we heard. The voices were getting closer, and we had to find Levy. After we had crawled for a minute, we stopped and I hooted once more. A few seconds later, a whippoorwill responded to our left, and I knew that it was Levy. We crawled as fast as we could to him and found him lying against a fallen tree.

"Stay low, we have to move!" he said as we approached him. We could hear the men splashing through the water as they were coming our way. "Okay, boys, on three, we are all going to stand up and run. If you don't get up and run, I give you my word that you will be left behind." Before he got to three, I jumped up and ran as fast as I could. I could hear Levy and Joe to my right as the shots began to ring out behind us. The bullets shrieked past me, hitting the trees all around me. It was too late to turn and fight. We needed to get the group back together before we engaged McCrae's men.

I ran until I heard Levy whistle, and when I made my way over to him and Joe, he pulled me to the ground. In between shots, Levy hooted again, and someone answered close. We stayed as low as we could and made our way over to the noise, where we found the three brothers, Olomill and Obadiah. "Where is Tobias?" Levy asked. Obadiah looked to the ground and just shook his head.

"Unfortunately, he did not make it, but we need to move," Randall said. Levy was stunned, but he quickly recovered and urged us to follow him. As Randall walked behind Levy, he said, "It sounds like a dozen guns or so. If we dig in and fight, we might overtake them. They don't know we are armed yet. We ain't fired a shot!"

Levy stopped, turned toward Randall, and said, "Oh, we are going to fight. We need to lead them where we want them first. I'm putting an end to this today."

We continued on, with my adrenaline carrying me through the swamp. From that moment forward, I knew there was no avoiding a fight. I asked myself if Levy preferred fighting over getting out safely. I reckon he was tired of running, and he knew it would only get worse. He and Pa had talked of cutting the head off the snake before it could strike with full force. If that wasn't the time, then I don't believe there ever would have been a time. What had to be done called for a man who was hardened by the stripes on his back and the scars on his heart. It called for someone who wasn't afraid to step out of line.

Levy was fueled by the rage that he had stored up inside. I imagined that every beating that he had received from Pierce and Will McCrae played back in his mind. His veins seemed as if they were going to burst through his skin, and sweat dripped from his nose. He was clearly consumed by revenge. Pa always told me not to back a fighter into a corner because, though he may lose, I would have to kill him, and what it would take to accomplish that may be too costly. Simply put, if a man isn't ready to die for what he believes in, then he had better not step out of line with someone who is.

Levy was ready to bring it all to an end and raise his family like every other free man had the privilege of doing, whatever the cost may be. Anyone he had to lose now, except Joe, rested comfortably in Montgomery. I knew

Levy would keep an eye on Joe, but whether they knew it or not, that is the main reason I had travelled to the swamp and defied my father. I had grown to love Joe like a brother during a time when I had lost my own. Brothers do unto others as they would have others do unto them. Harrisons weren't ones to turn and run from a tail whipping, especially if it involved protecting someone that we loved.

We followed Levy through the palmettos and thickets until he finally stopped. We were all gasping for air as the men kept pushing forward and coming in our direction. The light from their lanterns danced in the darkness like fireflies as they obviously had no intention of hiding from anyone. They were there to do one thing, and one thing only. We were all that stood between them and many, many lost lives. Levy preached that to us as he led us over a small ridge and into a clearing.

The moon provided the only light that we had. On the other side of the small clearing was a ditch, and that is where we finally hunkered down. It was an excellent spot to lay low and remain protected from incoming bullets. We all had a comfortable rest as we waited for McCrae's men to crest over the hill. "Wait for my command to shoot!" Levy said as the lights from the lanterns became brighter.

I pulled the hammer back on the .44 magnum lever action and prayed for safety under my breath. The brothers were cool and collected as they steadied their rifles. Joe was focused on Levy and waiting for the command to drop the hammer on the men who had torn his family apart. Olomill and Obadiah were about like me, anxious to stay alive and making the best of the situation they found themselves in.

The first light crested the hill straight out from us, but the next light was much further to the left than we had anticipated. Then, on our right, another light appeared. The first three came over the hill ahead of the rest of the men. Levy said, "Randall, y'all take the one on the left, Joe and I will shoot the one in the middle, and Pat, y'all handle the one on the right." I could not think straight as the men were now becoming visible in the clearing. Was this really about to happen?

Each step that they took was a step closer to their death. They did not know that, but I knew that because my rest was firm and comfortable. The bead on the end of my barrel was locked on the approaching man's chest. Out of the corner of my eye, I saw the second wave of men coming over the hill. In a calm and steady voice, Levy said, "Let em' have it, boys!" The men could not have been more than twenty yards away, and we cut loose on them.

The first three men immediately folded and rolled down the hill towards us. By the time I aimed for the second wave of men, they had scattered like flies. It was a free-for-all all at that point as we all shot as much as possible, as fast as possible. Without having lanterns to focus on, the light from the surrounding gunfire privived the only source of light for aiming. As McCraes' men hurried to get back across the hill and out of sight, Randall yelled, "I got one or two of em'! I know I did!" I was certain that I had done the same, but at that moment, I couldn't speak.

The men attempted to return fire from the top of the ridge, but we were too steady and kept them pushed back. They had greatly underestimated the people they were hunting, and it was obvious that they weren't used to anyone firing back at them. As the men disappeared and everything went quiet, we had no choice but to listen to the sounds of the dying men before us. Randall offered to finish them off, but Levy urged him to save the ammunition.

Levy yelled, "Pierce! You coward! Are you going to fight or hide up there all night?" Pierce replied by sending a bullet down the hill that nearly met its mark. We all saw the muzzle blast and focused on that as we fired back.

"I reckon he heard you!" Luke said as he and Isaac laughed hysterically and continued firing up the hill. When the shooting stopped, Levy knew that he had gotten his answer from Pierce.

All night, we fired back and forth, hoping that the other side would eventually run out of bullets. We took turns keeping watch as we knew that Pierce could possibly try to flank us in the dark. My ears were ringing, I could not feel my feet, and my hands were burned from handling the hot rifle. Eventually, Levy agreed to keep watch and let us rest.

Some time later, I was awakened by the sound of gunfire on the ridge. When I sat up in the ditch, I saw Levy, Joe, and Olomill, but I no longer saw the three brothers or Obadiah. Five shots had rung out and somehow, Olomill was still sleeping beside Levy. I crawled down the ditch and shook Olomill to wake him up, but he did not move. Before I could shake him again, Levy said, "Pat! He's gone! He died while you were asleep."

My heart sank as I rolled Olomill over and saw the blood and gunshot wound in his chest. "I never got to say goodbye to him," I said.

Levy sighed, "None of us did. He must have been shot before we took cover, and he never told any of us. He just kept fighting. I'm not sure when he passed." I had formed a relationship with Olomill, and what began as sadness quickly turned into anger.

It was now early morning, but the visibility was still low. I studied my burned and blistered hands while wondering how I would be able to carry on. "What about Obadiah and the brothers? Where did they go?" I asked Levy.

"The brothers volunteered to sneak around the ridge and see how many of McCrae's men were left. I fear that they may have just met their demise." Deep down, I knew that losing the brothers would be a devastating blow. They were fearless and obviously the right men for the job.

"What about Obadiah?" I asked.

"I sent him home after we realized Olomill was gone. He snuck away in the dark, and I'm going to give you the same opportunity, Pat."

"You think that I am going back?"

"You and Joe are free to do as you please. There has been enough death already, and this fight is between Pierce and me."

Joe spoke up and said, "That is where you are wrong, Pop. They stole you out of my life, and I know what he did to Mama. I was there, too. I want to see this through."

Levy said, "No matter what happens to me, when daybreak comes, keep your heads down and make sure you get out of here alive."

A voice called out from up the hill, "Levy, it's been a while since I killed a couple of white men! How many more are down there with you? How many more have to die before you give up?"

Levy yelled, "We aren't giving up, Pierce! There are a couple more white men who need to be held accountable first."

"Are you sure you are the man for that job?"

"Oh, I think I've proved that before!"

An awkward silence followed, and then Pierce said, "Ain't but two of us left up here, and I'm out of bullets! If you hate me so much, why don't we settle it like men, right here, right now? No weapons, just me and you!"

Levy yelled, "I know you're lying, you snake!"

Pierce responded, "I'll prove it to you!"

Moments later, we saw the large figure come over the ridge while holding his rifle in one hand, above his head. He threw his rifle on the ground and said, "Come on, let's go! This has been a long time coming!"

Joe cried, "Pop, no." But Levy ignored his wishes and quickly jumped out of the ditch.

Before he walked away, he said, "I don't trust that man. Both of you stay ready, and if anyone tries anything, cut them down."

Levy confidently walked out into the clearing with nothing but a knife on his side. Pierce lumbered down the hill like a grizzly bear itching for a fight. The two men met in the middle of the clearing and stood only ten feet apart. Joe and I carefully rested our rifles, aiming for Pierce's rotten heart. Pierce said to Levy, "I thought I said no weapons, you better get rid of that knife, boy."

Levy replied, "I'm not your boy, boy," as he pulled the knife from his side and tossed it in our direction.

"Will, he had a knife on him! Why don't you come out here and make sure that he doesn't try anything? We want to keep this a fair fight. Right, Levy?" Then Will McCrae, the son of the man who had caused all of this, topped the hill and eased down with a rifle in his hands. Joe and I quickly stood and jumped out of the ditch. We walked around and sat at the base of the tree Levy and Joe had been using for cover. We kept our eyes on Will as he took a knee on the side of the hill. The stage was then set for the two men to seek revenge on each other.

Pierce and Levy began to slowly walk in a circle as they sized each other up. Pierce said, "Oh, I've been meaning to ask, how is Lucy? I sort of miss her company."

Levy snapped and charged Pierce before he stopped and put his hands up in a fighting position. Levy swung first and connected, but Pierce ate the punch and gave one back, slowing Levy's advance. Then the two men locked up and rolled on the ground as they grunted and attempted to gain control of each other.

Levy was much quicker and in much better shape. He worked around Pierce and got on top of him. He attempted to drive Pierce's head deeper into the soil with each punch. I could hear his fists and Pierce's hard head connecting with the ground. "This is about how it went the first time," Joe said, as we watched. Levy was like a machine, and he was too much for Pierce to handle.

After he embarrassed Pierce, he invited him to get up so that he could further humiliate him. Pierce slowly stood, spat and wiped the blood from his nose. Levy advanced again, and he and Pierce exchanged blows. It was clear that Pierce was getting tired at this point, but he was still defending himself. Levy worked circles around him as Pierce grabbed Levy, pulling him to the ground. They rolled on the ground for what seemed like forever, each of them gasping for air.

Levy eventually got the upper hand again and started to work on Pierce. Will stood and began to act nervously as he realized his counterpart was losing the fight. Joe and I kept an eye on him and dared him to make a move. Then something happened, and Levy lost his momentum. "He's got a knife!" he screamed as I could see Pierce repeatedly attempting to stab Levy in his side.

My eyes immediately went back to Will, who was now locked on Joe and me with his rifle. "What do we do, Pat?" Joe asked, as Levy slowly rolled off Pierce and onto the ground.

"Just stay on McCrae. If he flinches, shoot him!" Pierce slowly stood and wiped the blood from the blade of his knife as he hovered over Levy. My heart sank, and I felt that this was the end for Levy.

Pierce kicked Levy in the ribs where he had been stabbing him and screamed, "I told you that your day was coming, nigger!"

Joe and I remained locked on Will as he remained locked on us. I knew that if I swung my rifle and shot Pierce, Will would likely shoot Joe or possibly both of us. I felt like our only option was to wait for a miracle. Time was running out as Pierce sat on top of Levy, preparing to take his revenge.

Pierce beat Levy with everything that he had, and Levy went unconscious. Pierce, huffing for air, grabbed his knife with both hands and raised it over his head as Levy lay under him. It was now or never, and neither Joe nor I knew what to do. Out of nowhere, a shot rang out from behind us, and a red mist of blood painted the bank behind Pierce. His hands dropped, then he fell over, on top of Levy. Will swung his rifle to take aim at whoever had taken the shot, but before he could find his target, Joe and I both shot. The bullets met their mark as Will hunched over and rolled down the hill.

Joe yelled, "Pop!" and we took off running toward Levy. We rolled Pierce's body off Levy and saw the blood that stained his shirt. Pierce was still alive, somehow with a bullet hole through his chest. Levy struggled to get up and then picked Pierce's knife up out of the sand. He said, "Boys, turn around. I don't want you to see this," and he took what remained of Pierce's life.

Levy then asked, "Who took that shot?" and before we could answer, I heard footsteps behind me. I turned to see my father, Doc, with a rifle in his hands and tears in his eyes. Pa had saved Levy's life with a crack shot from a long distance.

Looking up to heaven, he said, "It's all over now. Lord, please forgive us all. Please! Forgive us, Father!"

18

REVIVAL

Pa said, "You are lucky, Levy. Had he gotten that blade in a little deeper, we wouldn't be talking right now." Levy had several deep cuts along his side, but thankfully, no fatal stab wounds.

"It sure felt like it cut deep! How did you find us anyway, Doc?"

"Oh, you weren't hard to find. I just followed the sound of the shots."

Then Joe asked Pa, "How long have you been out here?"

"Long enough to know that Pierce had something up his sleeve, and it looks like I was right," Pa answered.

Pa removed his shirt and wrapped it firmly around Levy and his wounds. Levy's left eye was swollen shut, and his face was battered. He and Pa leaned over Pierce, studying his dead body as a mixture of blood and sweat fell from Levy's face to the ground. "I hate that it came to this, Levy."

"Me, too, but the man wasn't going to stop, Doc."

"I know he wasn't, and though it is unfortunate, he gave us no choice," Pa said.

I never knew if Pa or Levy had killed a man before that, but Joe and I surely hadn't. By the time it was over, we had become killers. The men who were on the other end of our rifles were more like animals than people, but did they deserve to die? I told myself that we could not stand by and allow more lives to be lost, but we had just taken lives ourselves. I wrestled with this in the days to come.

As I studied Pierce's lifeless body, I felt nothing. Just days before, I fantasized about someone putting him in his place. Now, someone would be putting him in the ground. It had all come to a head, and I was just glad that it wasn't Levy lying there. Pa spoke up, "Where are the three brothers?"

Levy answered, "Last we saw them, they went up that ridge in the dark. We heard shots at daylight before Pierce walked out."

"I ran into Obadiah on the way in, and he said Tobias didn't make it. What about Olomill?" Pa asked.

Levy pointed, "He's right over there in that ditch. We think he was shot before we took cover, but he kept fighting like he wasn't hit. I told the boys to get some rest, and I believe he died in his sleep. When we tried to wake him up, he was already gone." Pa hung his head and began to weep before he cautiously approached the ditch.

He gently eased into the ditch and placed his hand on Olomill's head. "He didn't say anything? Why would he keep quiet?" Pa asked.

Joe answered, "I knew Olomill better than anyone, and I bet it was because he was convinced that he didn't have much to live for. He knew his mama and sisters were gone. He was stubborn as a mule, but he knew why we were out here, and he wanted to end all of this as much as any of us."

Pa said, "He played an important role in all of this. It really all started with him. He was of great value, whether he knew that or not. He will be missed." Pa then climbed out of the ditch and approached Will McCrae's body. "I thought that was Will," he said as he shook his head. "It didn't have to come to this, Will."

Pa began walking up the ridge, shouldering his rifle. He crept up slowly as Joe, Levy and I followed. We had not been on the top side yet, and though it had been quiet, Pa wasn't taking any chances. When he reached the top, he paused and then lowered his rifle. What I saw on top of that ridge would stick with me forever.

When we topped the hill, there were dead bodies scattered about. The only three that we recognized were the brothers. In all, there were eleven deceased members of Pierce's crew, and six of them were on top of the ridge. "The brothers did some damage, I reckon," Pa said. When we walked up, the brothers were just feet from each other. Randall, Isaac, and Luke had all died from gunshot wounds, but not before they were able to take six of Pierce's men with them.

The two McCrae men who were lying closest to Isaac and Luke still had knives buried in their chests. Just hours before, I had watched as the brothers sharpened those same knives and prepared them for battle. It looked as if Randall was attempting to make his way to Pierce when he was gunned down. The three brothers had been fearless and so full of life that to see them lying there was a shock to us all.

Pa told Joe and me to go get the horses and bring two of them back as quickly as possible. Levy tried to stand and help, but Pa wouldn't let him get up. He told Levy to stay behind while he went and got his own horse. "You stay there. You've already lost enough blood."

"You know which way we are going?" Joe asked.

"Yeah, let's go. Follow me!" I replied. By the time Joe and I made it halfway back to camp, we were both soaking wet and exhausted. When I placed my hand on a tree to rest for a moment, I could see where the bullets had ripped bark from the tree. Then I heard Joe yelling, "Pat, over here! It is Tobias!"

Lying in the green palmettos was the body of Tobias. The flies were already swarming around him as I grabbed his legs and pulled him out into the open. Joe began to get sick and had to walk away for a moment. It was a gruesome sight as it was obvious he had been shot above his right eye. I imagined that he was killed during the first few moments when Pierce and his crew opened fire on us. He was no more than twenty yards from the water's edge.

"Come on, Joe. We are almost there!" I assured him. Then we left Tobias's body behind and crossed the swamp. After we made it back to the camp and caught our breath for a moment, we tied the horses together and cautiously led them back through the swamp and cypress knees. I followed the muddy path that we had previously created until we finally made it back to Pa and Levy.

Pa had already dragged all of the bodies together at the top of the ridge and was sitting beside Levy when we rode up.

"Y'all get down and come join us," Pa said. Joe and I dismounted and walked over to where they were sitting. Pa asked us to help Levy stand, and we all walked over to where the three brothers were lying. "I want to say a prayer for these young men who gave their lives for something bigger than themselves. If it weren't for them, each one of us could be dead. Let's go to the Lord in prayer."

Pa continued, "Father, I'm not sure if this is the outcome you wanted from all of this. What I do know is that we are thankful for these three young men. We thank you for their lives and for sending them to help bring an end to all of this mess. Father, we ask for forgiveness for our part in this. Thank you for protecting Levy, Joe, and Pat, and thank you for your guidance. We pray for understanding, closure, and most of all, peace. Help us to make the right decisions in the future and be a light for your kingdom. Amen."

When Pa was done praying, I noticed that Levy was emotional and crying. Levy said, "Look at all of this death around us! I can't do it anymore, Doc. I'm tired of running. I'm tired of fighting. I'm tired of taking the short end of the stick! All of this happened because I was bent on revenge! This was supposed to be between me and Pierce. I've been blinded by rage and fueled by revenge. I don't even recognize myself anymore."

Pa rushed to Levy's side and said, "Levy, my story isn't the same as yours, but I know how you feel. The only way to get rid of that extra weight is to give it all to Jesus. We have to surrender all of that to him and allow him to work on us. We can't do it on our own. Trust me, I know."

"I just don't understand all of that, Doc. All of the bad things that I've done on top of this mess, ain't no way that Jesus still wants me!"

Pa smiled, "Yes, he does. God not only loves you, but he loves you so much that he sent his only son to die for you."

"What do you mean?" Levy asked.

"Yeah, those sins that you are referring to, Jesus died for those sins. That's how much he loves you! When we are born again in baptism, he remembers our sins no more."

Levy sat in silence and deep thought with tears running down his face. The adrenaline had completely worn off, and we were all exhausted, but something else had a hold on Levy. I hadn't seen him like this since I had met him, and I don't think Joe had ever seen him like this either. He broke the silence and said, "So, you are telling me that all I have to do is get dunked in the water, and every bad thing I have ever done will go away? That sounds more like magic than anything, Doc."

Pa quickly responded, "That's not exactly how it works. When we accept Christ, we are called to be set apart and to live differently. We read God's Word, and that is what tells us how to live. We don't always get it right, but we are forgiven in Christ. Once we follow him, our desires change, and we become a new creation."

"I don't know if I am ready for all of that," Levy quietly said.

Pa looked around at our surroundings and said, "Well, if there's ever going to be a time, it looks like you are dang close to it." Pa stood and patted Levy on the back as he said, "Alright, let's get these boys back to the house and go get Levy fixed up."

"Wait, Pa, what about these other men? Are we just going to leave them out here?"

"Pat, these men are not my responsibility. I hate that they died, but they knew what they were signing up for. I've said my prayers for them, and what Angus decides to do with them is his business. Do you want to be the one to go tell Angus McCrae that his son is dead, along with Pierce and his posse? No? Well, I can't ask anyone else to do that either." I figured Pa was right, but something sure felt wrong about it.

Joe and I placed Olomill and the brothers on horseback as Pa went over to bid farewell to Tobias. Then, we assisted Levy with mounting his horse, and we slowly made our way out of the swamp. I felt relieved to know that it was all over, but we had paid a heavy price for it. People had lost their lives, and Joe and I had lost our innocence. Out of curiosity, I rode up beside Pa and asked, "So, how bad is it gonna be?"

"How bad is what going to be?" he asked.

"The butt-whipping that you have planned for me. How bad is it gonna be?"

Pa smirked, "I haven't thought that far ahead yet."

I couldn't help myself, so I asked, "How did you know that I was gone anyway?"

"Well, son, next time you want to sneak out, you'd better think it through a little better. When I heard the first shots, I came to your room. It wasn't hard to tell whatever you stuffed under those blankets wasn't my son. I knew where you had gone.

"Pat, I'm disappointed that you disobeyed me, but I'm also proud of you for standing up for something that you believe in. You knew that you should not have come out here, and you knew the danger that came along with it. In this situation, you are right and wrong, but fortunately for you, the good outweighs the bad. I can't punish you for protecting the people that you love. The reason I didn't come out here with Levy was that I did not want to do something that I would regret, but it is too late for that. At the same time, if I hadn't come out here to watch out for you, Levy would likely be dead. So, you see, we both find ourselves in a very similar predicament. The only thing we can do is pray and ask God for understanding and wisdom."

I can't describe the amount of relief that I felt when Pa told me that. I had been there for my best friend and survived, and Pa wasn't going to hold it over my head. I honestly think that I was more worried about facing my father than I was about facing Pierce and his crew. We were on to greener pastures, and it felt like the storm was passing.

Pa led us to the cemetery where we had buried my brother and grandfather. When we stopped, Pa said, "I'm going to go get my medical kit and a few shovels. I'll be right back."

As he rode toward the house, Levy said, "When Randall asked to be buried here, I didn't take him seriously. I thought we were all going to make it out alive. They didn't have to die for me."

Joe said, "Don't be so hard on yourself, Pop. We all knew what we were getting into. It is not all your fault." I looked around at the beautiful cemetery and wondered how many times someone had stood there and wept. I thought about how many people stood there and blamed themselves for the death of someone they loved. After Levy rid himself of the rage that was living inside of him, it was obvious that he was having a hard time living with the consequences. I could see that he felt their blood was on his hands.

Honestly, none of it had gone like I thought it would. I figured Joe and I would be laughing and swapping stories. I thought we might brag to each other about protecting what was ours. As we sat under the towering pecan trees, that is not at all the feeling that consumed us. There was sadness, and the reality of what had just taken place was heavy on our shoulders.

When Pa made it back to the cemetery, he was followed by a large crowd of people coming out to see what had happened to Levy. Tildy broke away from the crowd and jumped onto Joe, wrapping her arms and legs around him. As they embraced, she said, "We heard the shots, and I thought that I had lost you!"

Joe replied, "No, ma'am. I told you that I would make it back to you." If there were any doubts that the two of them were in love, that moment brought an end to that discussion. Everyone else stood around studying the bodies while Pa began to clean Levy's wounds.

Milly, a gentle older woman, walked over and sat beside Levy in the grass. She said, "Levy, you have sacrificed so much. You have risked your life for all of us, and I want you to know how grateful we are. I'm glad you made it back to us."

Levy quietly said, "Thank you, Milly, but what about the ones that didn't make it back?" He pointed to the bodies lying across from them under the pecan tree.

"I know it's hard, but if you need anything, just tell me," Milly said as she walked away.

Obadiah looked at Tobias, Olomill, and the brothers and wept, "I should have stayed out there! I never should have left when Levy gave me the choice." Fannie Mae walked over to comfort Obadiah, but he took one of the shovels and began ferociously attacking the ground and digging. Some of the older children came over and gave Obadiah a hand.

Pa called everyone together, saying, "Before we bury these men, I want to share a word with you and honor their lives. They deserve that. None of us wished for any of this to happen. Angus McCrae and his men were not going to stop, and you all know the violence that they are capable of. Unfortunately, we had to resort to violence to protect you all and ourselves.

"Levy was cut up pretty good, but he made it back. Sadly, as you can see, Olomill, Tobias, Randall, Isaac, and Luke were not so fortunate. They all fought bravely and died with honor. They died protecting you, and they did it without hesitation. Now that all of this is over, I want to make my intentions clear to everyone.

"Whether you came from the McCrae place or whether you came from Bellewood, I want you to know that you are welcome to stay here. I know that the war is over, and you know that I've never supported slavery. You are free to go and do as you please, but if you remain here, we will serve the Lord and do things the right way. What you work for will be yours. I do not wish to profit from your hard work, but you will be treated fairly and honestly. I want everyone to understand one thing: not all white men are like James Smith and Angus McCrae.

"Now, we are going to lay these bodies to rest today and honor these fine men." Joe, Obadiah, and I carefully placed the bodies in the holes, and they began to cover them up. Pa continued, "In the Book of John, chapter fifteen, verse thirteen, it says, 'Greater love hath no man than this, that a man lay down his life for his friends.' " I thought about the bravery of each man lying there as Pa preached. It fit our current situation perfectly, and it brought us all peace knowing the sacrifices that they made out of love.

When Pa finished, Old Bob stepped forward, "The man is telling the truth. I thought I was a dead man until he baptized me in the creek! After that, I have felt more peace than I ever have!

Then Obadiah came forward, "I saw how it was out there. I was in the middle of it. Doc, I think I am ready to know Jesus and get baptized like Bob did. I've lost my best friend and my family. I need the peace that Bob is talking about."

Pa happily said, "Obadiah, I would be honored to baptize you."

I could tell that Levy wanted to say something, but he fought it off and remained quiet. Pa went on saying, "Baptism makes it public that a person wants to repent of their sins and follow Jesus. They cross over from death to life just like Joshua led the Israelites across the Jordan River."

Obadiah spoke up and asked, "Where was the Jordan River, Doc?"

"It is a place in Israel in which Jesus Christ himself was baptized by John the Baptist. It is where Elijah and Elisha crossed over and where they say the water is blessed," Pa said.

Obadiah proudly replied, "Well, they have the Jordan River, but we have the creek!"

Just then, Levy could not take it anymore, he belted out, "I am ready too!"

Pa asked, "What did you say, Levy?"

Levy stuttered, "I think that I am ready, too."

Then Joe stood up, "Me, too." All around us, people started saying that they were ready to be baptized.

"Praise God! It sounds like we need to make a trip to the creek this evening!" Pa said as he looked at me and smiled.

All day, Pa gathered with and talked to each person who decided they wanted to be baptized. He shared the gospel with them and gave them Bibles that he had saved up from the church. For him, it was a dream come true. He was surrounded by people who were hungry for Jesus. They wanted a one-way ticket out of the hell that they had been through, and Jesus was the only way. Among the people who made the decision were Levy, Obadiah, Joe, Milly, Hannah, Minerva, Mary, Tildy, Fannie Mae, and, surprisingly, old ornery Eadys.

Later that afternoon, when it had cooled down some, we all made our way to the creek. The ones that had made the decision stood on the sandbar as the rest of the crowd watched from above.

Pa had led us to a beautiful spot where it was clean and crystal clear. With the light fading, he called Obadiah out into the water. Obadiah proudly walked into the cool water and made his way over to Pa.

Pa said, "You know what we talked about today and what this means."

Obadiah replied, "Yes, sir, I am ready."

"Upon your profession of faith, I now baptize you in the name of the Father, the Son, and the Holy Spirit." He dipped Obadiah under and brought him back up as everyone applauded and cheered from up above.

Obadiah made his way out of the water while cheering and engaging the onlookers. He shouted, "We've got our own River Jordan!"

"Who is next?" Pa asked.

Joe stepped forward and said, "I'll go next, but I want Pat to be the one to do it." I froze and asked why he wanted me to do it. "Well, you've been baptized before, right?" I nodded. "Well, come on then." Pa urged me to come into the water as I passed the lantern I was holding to Levy.

The water was colder than I expected, but it didn't faze any of us. I met Joe where Pa had just baptized Obadiah, and I asked, "Joe, are you ready to be baptized, and do you know what this means?"

"Yes, I am ready to serve Jesus." Tildy was elated and cheering Joe on from the creek bank.

I said, "I baptize you in the name of the Father, the Son, and the Holy Spirit." His face disappeared under the water, and I felt him grab my arms to pull himself back up. After Joe came out of that water, he was never the same. I loved him before, but after that day, we became brothers in Christ. He hugged me with tears in his eyes and thanked me for our friendship. It was one of the most special moments of my life.

After I baptized Joe, he turned around and baptized Levy, cementing a firm bond between his Heavenly Father and his earthly father. Then he baptized Tildy. The others who had made the decision requested to be baptized by Levy. They had crossed over the Jordan and were on their way to the Promised Land. We stayed until after dark, baptizing by the light of the lantern and the power of the Holy Spirit.

When the last person, Minerva, emerged from the water, we all cheered and clapped. A few of the women started singing, and then we all chimed in and joined hands. The most significant thing in all our lives had just taken place, and the tides had turned. We had all experienced the lowest of lows, but in that moment together dancing and singing alongside the creek, we experienced the highest of highs. The fiery dart of division that Satan had sent our way had been deflected by the love of Jesus Christ and a group of people who decided to trust and have faith in him.

19

After the first baptisms, I remember the Holy Spirit moving at Bellewood. It was like God was replacing everything that the enemy had stolen. Each day, it seemed like someone different decided to be baptized in the Pintlala Creek. When everyone had gone, more came. They came from all over Lowndes County and from different plantations. Word spread quickly of the revival that had taken place on our farm.

The previous slaves that were local to the area began referring to the creek as "Our River Jordan." Before Milly, Hannah, Obadiah, and Fannie Mae left the farm, they carved the words "Our River Jordan" deep into a board. They took the sign to the original baptism's location and placed it by a cottonwood tree. That beautiful place that my father was led to on the creek became a very special place for a great many people.

We baptized more people than I could count. Black and white, both came to be baptized in the same water. Bellewood became like a bubble, and inside that bubble, racism and prejudice were not accepted or tolerated. From the outside, there were voices of doubt and anger. On the inside, we were focused on one thing, and that was to share the gospel with as many people as possible.

Some loved it and some hated it, but no one stopped it. There were attempts to protest and riot, but once Grandpa Lewis arrived with the lawmen, that stopped. When he placed armed guards at the gate, for some reason, those angry folks weren't as angry anymore. There were a few local families that did not approve of what was happening, but we did not listen to the outside voices.

Grandpa Lewis and Grandma Jane finally, thankfully, brought my mother, Lucy and Nan home to us. Before they departed for Montgomery, Grandpa and the lawmen decided to make a stop by Angus McCrae's and let him tell his side of the story. According to Grandpa, that didn't work out well for Angus in his old age.

Afterward, Grandpa Lewis told my father that Angus had tried to buy the lawmen off. When they did not accept his offer, he refused to be taken in for further questioning. Grandpa watched as Angus attempted to pull a revolver from his waist as the men tried to detain him. In self-defense, the lawmen shot him down. In his own office, where he had previously claimed that there was no law, he died at the feet of the law.

Around that time, everyone who didn't have intentions of staying on the farm had already left. Pa eventually attempted to send the McCrae prisoner, sixteen-year-old Frenchman David Tenequen, away. David firmly denied the offer and stated that he wanted to stay on our property for a while and learn how to farm. He had become best friends and bunk mates with old Eadys, who had previously beaten him with a whip. I guess the Lord does work in mysterious ways.

Eadys was old, hardened, and bitter before he took a dip in the creek, but in his last few years, he softened up and told stories of the old days to the children. We all grew to love him, and he went to be with the Lord in

1869. We buried him under the pecan tree beside Olomill. Oddly enough, I think it was hardest on David, who had grown to love Eadys. Often in the afternoons, David would go spend time in the pecan grove and talk with Eadys. We didn't know much about David besides the fact that he didn't have any family in America and that he lacked a father figure in his life. I think, in a short amount of time, Eadys filled that role.

With the help of my Grandpa Lewis, my father and Levy started their own farming operation. They split the profits down the middle and worked from daylight to dark nearly every day. They planted corn and cotton by hand, and they trapped fur-bearing animals on the creek. We never were rich after the war, but Pa and Levy always provided for us, and they made sure that Joe and I pulled our weight as well.

After a couple of years of Joe's family living in Lucy's cabin, we helped them build a home on the other side of the swamp. It sits where our previous home was located before Wilson's raid. Levy had saved up enough money to buy the materials, and we worked for free, of course. Grandpa Lewis came and stayed with us at Bellewood so that he could oversee the project. People are still in awe when they see the beauty of the home today.

Levy finally had what he dreamed of having. He was no longer separated from his family, and they were starting over. Previously, I had heard him talk about making those dreams become reality, and it was a blessing to watch him walk it out. He was a good husband, a hard worker, an honest man, and an exceptional father. After that spring, he did an outstanding job raising Joe and Nan. Little by little, Levy won Nan's heart, and she accepted him as her father.

After Levy truly got on his feet, our farming operation took off. It was hot, back-breaking work, but we did it alongside our best friends, so it always felt more like fun than work. One day, Joe and I got to ride to town with my father and Levy. They claimed that they had discovered a way to plant corn and cotton twice as fast as we normally did. For some reason, they wouldn't tell Joe what we were going to pick up.

When we arrived at Harris Seed and Supply in downtown Montgomery, I saw what my father had been ranting about. Outside the front doors, there were two shiny new Blair row planters sitting side by side. My father said that one was for planting corn and the other was for planting cotton. They looked like wheelbarrows, but dropped seed out of the bottom, and had rakes that gently covered the seeds with soil.

Henry Blair, an African American man, invented the corn row planter in 1834. After that, in 1836, he invented the cotton row planter. Blair was a free man from Maryland who used his ingenuity to save the backs of farmers all across the nation. We were proud to load up those planters and take them back to the farm.

We spent nearly every day of each spring and summer working in the hot sun. Though it was physically taxing, it was also rewarding to see the fruits of our labor and enjoy them together. Joe and I had always been close, but the relationship that we formed over the years was unbreakable. To this day, we are as close as brothers.

I reckon it's because of everything that we went through together. Nothing was ever strong enough to break our bond because it was founded on love and respect. We were always forgiving with each other and realized that the world treated us very differently. We were always there for one another and relied on God to carry our families and friendships. Over the years, we adopted the saying, "A man's word is his bond," and we taught that to our children.

So, when a man gets old, and he is on the backside of his life, what are the things that he should really appreciate? For me, it has been an earthly father who raised me to love everyone, no matter how different we may be. It was watching him walk it out on a daily basis. It was the relationships that were born from situations that could have gone very differently if my father hadn't allowed God to lead. I often think about what the alternative would have been had my father not known Jesus.

It wasn't until years later that Levy finally gave in and told Lucy about what happened in the swamp. My mother had her suspicions that something had happened. I believe it was because that spring changed my father and me. It didn't change us for the worse, but we were not the same people that we were beforehand. Mama often asked us about it, and she never got closure until Lucy told her. Lucy and my mother had become best friends, and they often kept up with us through their daily talks.

Now, I am fifty-two years old, and recently, I decided to dust off this old journal. When I thought of our story's importance, I talked to Joe about it. We agreed that our stories needed to be told, but we were not ready to share them with our children. We agreed that we would leave it up to the Lord. I told him where I am going to bury it, and if nobody ever finds it, the story will die along with us.

The spot that I have chosen to bury this journal is where I connect with the Lord. I come here often to spend time with him. I have learned that our family's treasure lies within this land as well as our hearts. God provided the creek in which so many people surrendered to Christ. When I look around this spot, all I see is how wonderful his creation is.

In a way, I appreciate the hard times we had because many good things came from the struggles, but there were also serious consequences. The tension with the McCrae family is something that has never been fixed. After Angus passed, his oldest son Edward, along with his wife and children, came up from Louisiana and took over the McCrae farm. We have steered clear of that family since then, but we have heard the rumors that they spread throughout the community.

If discovered, I pray that this journal is passed down from generation to generation in the Harrison and Jones families. I pray that the real, true story is shared with whoever is willing to listen and that it glorifies God. You see, the treasure is not in this chest; the treasure lies within this story. The secret to living a happy life is not money, gold, or diamonds. The secret is the love that we carry in our hearts, and it is no secret that Jesus is the only way for us to possess that unconditional love.

20

JOHN HARRISON AND JUNIOR JONES 1979

As Junior and I stared across the blazing fire and admired the beauty of the woods around us, we looked at each other and smiled in silence. We had been waiting for nearly fourteen years to share the story with our children. We knew that the two boys wrestling on the sandbar would always remember this story. After all, whether they knew it or not, they were about to become part of it.

When it comes to the Harrison and Jones families, we believe in tradition and fighting for what is right in God's eyes. Junior and I both knew if these boys were going to be raised like we were, then they needed to know the truth about our families. They needed to know how important a relationship with God is and how he kept our families together through things that were meant to rip us apart. The boys needed to know that their friendship would not exist if, through years, we hadn't chosen love and kept our eyes on Jesus. Levy and Thomas had both accepted Jesus, and it was time for them to be baptized in this creek, just like so many before them.

"Y'all boys ready for a story?" I asked. Neither of our boys acknowledged me as they grunted and tested each other's strength on the sandbar. I walked over and grabbed two sticks of firewood and threw it on the fire when I realized that I would need to be dramatic to get their attention. "Hey, Junior, toss me that shotgun. There's a big cottonmouth in the creek," I screamed, winking at Junior. He tossed me the gun over the fire, and I shot across the creek into the sandy bank.

Fire came from the end of the shotgun's barrel, the woods went silent, and the boys jumped up and ran in our direction. I said, "Now that I have your attention, y'all sit down and listen! This is what Junior and I have been waiting to share with you for all of these years." Junior attempted to contain his laughter when he saw the boys hurry over, but he was unsuccessful.

My son Levy was built just like the rest of us, average height and stout. He was just starting to fill out and gain some muscle. Thomas, on the other hand, reminded me of his grandfather, Sam. He was long and lean, but muscular like those before him. They were both good boys because Junior and I didn't give them much of a choice.

Thomas and Levy finally stopped picking at each other, and I said, "I brought an old journal that I have been keeping since I was your age, and I want to read it to both of you. This is the story of both of our families and how we are linked together by the past. Levy, this was your grandfather Pat's journal, and over the years, I have added our story in. This weekend, both of you are becoming a part of something greater than yourselves."

All night and into the early hours of the morning, I read the journal to the boys. They were focused and eager to learn. They had stuffed their faces with RC Colas and Moon Pies all night. Junior, on the other hand, was doing his best not to doze off and fall out of his chair. Every few minutes, I would reach over and tap him to wake him up. Eventually, to keep him awake, I handed the journal to him, and he began to read.

After deep discussions, the boy's questions, and saying everything that we ever wanted to say to each other, there was no time left for sleep. Pat's story was quite often interrupted by Junior and me when we would insert our personal accounts. We laughed, cried, and bonded with our boys like we never had before. We told the whole truth, and there were no stones left unturned. The boys had a firm grasp on who they were, where they came from, and how they got to that point.

Before we knew it, the woods began to wake up around us as daybreak approached. Junior and I both knew that it was time. Thomas and Levy had no idea what our intentions were before we arrived, but when they heard the story, they caught on. When Junior and I stood from our chairs and stretched, they knew it was time.

I asked, "Are you boys ready?"

Thomas replied, "We've been ready. We are waiting on y'all."

Junior and I laughed and invited the boys down to where the cold, white sand met the water. Junior looked around and said, "This is where it all happened, boys."

Dumbfounded, Levy asked, "Is this the exact spot?"

I replied, "We've been here all night. This is where hundreds of baptisms have taken place since eighteen sixty-five."

The boys looked around as we all imagined our ancestors standing in the same spot. It was a moment that none of us will ever forget. The presence of God was heavy, as his redeeming power flowed by in the clear water. I said, "Levy, before you, there was Doc, Pat, your Grandpa Henry, and me."

Junior proudly said, "Thomas, before you, there was Levy, Joe, your Grandpa Sam and me."

"And, now it's our turn," Levy said.

"Which one of us is going first?" Thomas asked. Junior and I decided that we would baptize our boys, side by side, at the same time. The boys raced into the creek, splashing Junior and me with the cold water. The familiar feeling of the wet sand between my toes and the cold water rushing up my legs was nostalgic. After all of the years and the many baptisms, I still felt something powerful when I made my way into those waters.

The boys, soaking wet and breathing hard, made it to Junior and me in the deeper water. We took them and guided them through the water until they were in the right spot. Junior prayed, "Lord, we thank you for this moment. We thank you for these boys and for our fathers before us. Also, we are thankful for this story and the connection between our two families. We've been through a lot, Lord, but you have been with us through it all. Thank you for the love that we have for one another. We know that you are here in this moment, and we ask that you bless these young men and build them up to be strong. Amen."

Together, Junior and I said, "I now baptize you in the name of the Father, the Son, and the Holy Spirit," as we slowly eased our sons down into the water. When they emerged from the water, we didn't cheer and applaud like Pat said they did, but we both enjoyed a long moment of silence with Thomas and Levy. They cried on our shoulders as the two tough, rambunctious teens became putty in Jesus's hands.

Later that same day, we were milling around and fishing on the sandbar. Junior and I stoked the fire and prepared venison burgers on a cast-iron skillet. The two rowdy boys had become quieter and reserved. They seemed to be deep in thought that morning. "I wish they were this quiet beforehand," Junior joked. I believe the reality of what had taken place was settling deep inside the boys.

"It's time to eat!" I yelled as Junior pulled the burgers from the skillet and placed them on buns. When Levy and Thomas came over, Junior asked, "Why have y'all been so quiet this morning?"

Thomas replied, "I guess all of this is just a lot to take in." Levy agreed as they began to eat their lunch in silence.

We spent the rest of that day and one more night at the creek. By the time Sunday rolled around, Thomas and Levy were ready to go home. After we woke up, we broke the tents down and packed up everything. "We've got to make it home in time to get ready for church," Junior reminded the boys. They were dragging their feet and complaining that we woke them up too early.

Once we got everything together and cleaned the sandbar, the four of us carried everything up the hill and to the trucks.

"Ah, man. I left my fishing pole down there. I knew that I was forgetting something. I'll be right back!" Levy said.

After a few minutes, we heard him yelling from down below us. "Dad, come here quick! Hurry!"

All three of us darted down the hill, and as we approached, Levy said, "Look at this! This is the tree that my fishing pole was leaning against!"

Junior and I looked at each other and shook our heads in disbelief. It had been covered and hidden for years. Junior and I thought we had shared everything with the boys, but there was one thing that we had forgotten. Thomas and Levy ripped the vines away from the tree until Thomas stopped and said, "It's all true!"

We studied the sign for a moment, and we all read aloud, "Our River Jordan".

ABOUT THE AUTHOR

Jackson Owen, born in 1990, was raised just south of Montgomery in the small community of Hope Hull, Alabama. If Jackson is not spending time with his family, he is in the woods, hunting and writing. He is the founder of Sacred Hunt, an outdoor Christian brand that focuses on sharing the gospel of Jesus Christ through the outdoors. He is a proud husband, father and business owner. He has had stories published by Mossy Oak and Turkey Hunter magazine.

BEHIND THE STORY

From left to right: Pascal Henry Owen Jr., Tom Jones,

Lewis Harrison Owen (mid 60's)

Bellewood

Col. Lewis Owen

Dr. Pascal Harrison Owen

Mary Smith Owen

Jane Harrison Owen

Writing of Dr. Pascal Harrison Owen